SHADOWS BEHIND THE SCREEN

by

Nicholas Okumu

Nicholas Okumu

P. O. Box 34657-00100, Nairobi, Kenya

Nicholas.okumu@live.com

www.drnicholasokumu.com

Self-Published Edition

2024

Copyright

Shadows Behind the Screen

Copyright © 2024 by Nicholas Okumu

Publisher:

Self-Published by Nicholas Okumu

Nairobi, Kenya

ISBN: 979-8-9911208-3-8

Cover design by Nicholas Okumu

Printed in Republic of Kenya

First Edition: 2024

Dedication

To my mother, Magdalene Achieng Okoth.

You were the one who introduced me to the world of books, fostering a love for reading that has shaped my life. Through the works of African greats like Chinua Achebe, Wole Soyinka, Elechi Amadi, and Ngugi wa Thiong'o, you opened my eyes to the richness of our culture and history. Your shared biographies of influential figures such as Nelson Mandela, Steve Biko, Jomo Kenyatta, and Malcolm X ignited my curiosity and inspired my creativity. Your guidance and wisdom are the foundations upon which this work is built. Thank you for everything.

Acknowledgments

I give thanks to God almighty for he is the giver of all that I have including the gift of writing. I acknowledge my family for the sacrifice of time that they give me to do all the work I do—from practicing medicine, running businesses, advocating for surgical access, to teaching. They are there through all the hits and misses. Your unwavering support and understanding make it all possible. Thank you for being my constant pillars of strength.

I would also like to extend my gratitude to my mentors and colleagues, whose guidance and collaboration have been invaluable. To my editors and publishers, your efforts have helped bring this book to life. Lastly, thank you to my friends and professional networks for your encouragement and support.

Foreword

Have you ever wondered if you live a life similar to those within your social circles? Does it ever cross your mind to imagine if your daily experiences have any resonance to your contemporaries? What does the real or imagined sight of the proverbial green grass trigger within you? Are you one of those people who can switch off from the digital age for long periods during the day without feeling left out or do you go into panic if you haven't logged into your socials for more than an hour at a time?

We live in an age where the digital realm is truly an extension of our reality. The allure of the online world is undeniable: connection, convenience, and endless possibilities. But as Nicholas Okumu's *Shadows Behind the Screen* starkly reveals, this digital utopia can be an addictive mirage, concealing a darker underbelly. Okumu, with his keen eye for societal intricacies, paints a vivid portrait of Nairobi, a metropolitan melting pot of tradition and modernity. Through the lens of a Dr. Andrew, we are thrust into a world where the familiar facade of the online self, masks a complex interplay of power, deception, and vulnerability.

This completely fictional book is a realistic exposition of how art imitates life and how life can imitate art. It tries to portray how fraught our interconnected world is with immeasurable dangers, and the double edges of excitement and caution that we must embody while in it. How can we draw on the real connections that the offline world gives us to navigate the online ones better?

Get immersed in this gripping tale and enjoy the ride, its thrills and its spills like I did.

Paul Angatia Kataka

Contents

Preface

"Shadows Behind the Screen" began as an exploration of the hidden dangers lurking in the digital world and evolved into a story that intertwines family, power, and deception. As a practicing surgeon, business owner, and advocate for surgical access, I've encountered numerous challenges and witnessed the complex interplay between personal ambitions and societal expectations. These experiences have significantly influenced the themes and characters in this book.

The story reflects a modern-day Nairobi, a city where traditional values and contemporary influences converge, creating a rich tapestry of life that is both vibrant and perilous. The protagonist's journey through this landscape, navigating the shadowy corridors of digital manipulation and family secrets, mirrors the struggles many face in balancing professional duties and personal lives.

Writing this book allowed me to delve into the darker aspects of human nature and the ethical dilemmas that arise when power is wielded without accountability. It is a cautionary tale about the allure of quick thrills and the consequences of underestimating the reach of those who operate in the shadows.

I owe a debt of gratitude to my family for their unwavering support and patience throughout the writing process. Their sacrifices have allowed me to pursue my various passions, and this book is a tribute to their love and encouragement.

I hope "Shadows Behind the Screen" not only entertains but also provokes thought and reflection on the hidden forces that shape our lives. May it serve as a reminder to remain vigilant and question the realities presented to us in an increasingly digital world.

Thank you for joining me on this journey.

Nicholas Okumu

Introduction

In today's digital age, the boundaries between our online and offline lives have become increasingly blurred. The internet offers endless possibilities, from instant connections through social media to the thrilling experiences found on dating apps. However, these conveniences also come with significant risks. "Shadows Behind the Screen" delves into the hidden dangers lurking in the digital world, exploring how the allure of quick thrills and instant gratification can mask more sinister intentions.

This book is set in the vibrant yet perilous landscape of modern-day Nairobi, a city where traditional values and contemporary influences converge. Our protagonist, Dr. Andrew, a successful surgeon, finds himself ensnared in a web of deceit and danger after a seemingly innocent foray into online dating. As he navigates this treacherous terrain, he uncovers a shadowy underworld where power, corruption, and manipulation reign supreme.

"Shadows Behind the Screen" is not just a tale of suspense and intrigue; it is also a reflection on the ethical dilemmas and complexities of human nature. It raises questions about trust, loyalty, and the lengths to which individuals will go to protect their secrets. Through Andrew's journey, readers are invited to consider the precarious balance between the excitement of the digital world and the very real dangers that lie beneath its surface.

The purpose of this book is to entertain while also provoking thought and reflection on the hidden forces that shape our lives. It serves as a cautionary tale about the perils of digital anonymity and the consequences of underestimating those who operate in the shadows. As you turn the pages, you will be drawn into a story that is as thrilling as it is thought-provoking, a reminder to remain vigilant and discerning in an increasingly interconnected world.

Thank you for embarking on this journey with me. May "Shadows Behind the Screen" keep you on the edge of your seat while also inspiring you to look deeper into the unseen dynamics of our digital age.

PROLOGUE

The Nairobi night was alive with its usual hum of activity. Street vendors hawked their wares, the sounds of laughter and music spilling from bars and restaurants, and the endless stream of traffic created a cacophony that was both chaotic and comforting. Amidst this vibrant cityscape, an undercurrent of darkness flowed unseen, a shadowy world that thrived in the gaps between the streetlights and within the depths of the internet.

Dr. Andrew Okumu sat at his kitchen table, the remnants of his breakfast spread before him. His wife, Sally, was engrossed in her phone, making deals and coordinating the many facets of the family business empire she had inherited. Their two teenage daughters, equally absorbed in their own digital worlds, barely acknowledged his presence. Despite his successful career as a surgeon and the financial security provided by his wife's wealth, Andrew felt a void. The excitement that had once driven him seemed to have evaporated, leaving behind a restless yearning for something more.

A recent conversation with his friend Larry replayed in his mind. Over a round of golf at the

15

Golf and Country Club, Larry had let slip that he was dating a young woman he had met online. Larry's newfound vitality and happiness had struck a chord with Andrew, igniting a spark of curiosity and envy. Could the thrill of a new conquest be the antidote to his growing ennui?

Andrew had taken the plunge, creating a profile on a popular dating app, complete with fake pictures and a fabricated persona. The rush of anticipation and the excitement of clandestine conversations had quickly become addictive. It was a dangerous game, but one that made him feel alive again.

Tonight, Andrew had arranged to meet one of his online matches at the trendy Amara Lounge in Kilimani. Her profile had captivated him with its blend of innocence and allure. As he prepared for the evening, dyeing his hair to mask the encroaching gray and dressing in clothes that made him appear younger, a sense of foreboding nagged at the edges of his consciousness. He pushed it aside, eager to escape the monotony that had become his life.

Little did he know, this seemingly innocent rendezvous would be the beginning of a nightmare. As Andrew stepped into the night, he was unaware that the shadows behind the screen held far more than the promise of excitement—they harbored dangers that would threaten everything he held dear.

In the quiet luxury of Runda, another part of the city, the wheels of a sinister plan were already in motion. The Architect, a mastermind hidden behind layers of anonymity, orchestrated her schemes with cold precision. Tonight's operation was just another move in a game where the stakes were high and the players often unaware of their roles.

As Andrew's path converged with the dark undercurrents of Nairobi's hidden world, the stage was set for a series of events that would unravel secrets, challenge loyalties, and blur the lines between victim and perpetrator. This is where our story begins—a tale of suspense, intrigue, and the delicate balance between the thrill of the digital age and the shadows that lurk beneath.

CHAPTER 1:

THE PRECIPICE OF CURIOSITY

It was a typical morning in the tranquil suburb of Karen, where the lush greens of the Karen Golf and Country Club were just a stone's throw away from my home. The morning light streamed through the expansive windows of our home, illuminating the opulence of a carefully curated lifestyle. The breakfast room, with its view of the meticulously landscaped gardens, was alive with the quiet hum of our household staff attending to their duties. The aroma of freshly brewed coffee blended with the subtle scent of blooming jacarandas from the garden, filling the air with a promise of serenity that only wealth could afford.

Over the breakfast table my family gathered. My wife, Sally, ever the picture of elegance, sat across from me, her beauty untouched by time but lately marred by the lines of stress that business demands etched softly upon her face. Despite the early hour, she was already absorbed in her phone, negotiating deals with a sharpness that was daily growing her family's empire. The wealth her family wielded wasn't just in the numbers; it was in the air we breathed, the 12-car garage housing a collection that included my Land Rover Defender—a symbol of rugged luxury that I took pride in driving. Her attention was buried in her phone, negotiating deals with the effortless grace of someone born into wealth. Her family's empire was vast and varied, its origins and operations shrouded in layers of business dealings that even I hadn't fully unraveled.

Sally had effectively taken the reins of her aging father's conglomerate. Despite having siblings, it was she who steered the ship, with a deftness that spoke of her inherent knack for business. Our daughters, both teenagers, were engrossed in their own worlds, fingers swiping through their phones, their conversations a series of emojis and laughter that seldom included me. A silence had settled between Sally and me—a chasm widened by unspoken words and the growing distance her business had created between us.

Amid the buzz of family life, I sat with my tablet, scrolling through the news, feeling a pang of ennui. As a successful surgeon, my life was ostensibly fulfilling, but the magnitude of Sally's wealth made my achievements feel diminished. She had once asked me to leave my practice, to travel the world with her and perhaps find peace in leisure. But pride had held me back. I was too ingrained in my identity as a provider, too set in my ways to become what I feared most—a kept man, adrift on his wife's fortunes. Yet there was a growing itch for something... different. The thrill of the operating room had become routine, and the comfort of financial security, courtesy of both my career and Sally's wealth, left me craving a spark of excitement, a deviation from the norm. Surrounded by the trappings of success—from the premium membership at the exclusive Golf and Country Club to the silent acknowledgment by our uniformed staff as they went about their tasks—I felt an inexplicable void.

I recalled a conversation with my friend Larry during a recent round of golf at the Country Club. He had seemed unusually upbeat, almost rejuvenated, and when I prodded, he confessed to dating someone new, a younger woman he'd met online. "It's a different world out there, exciting and a bit addictive," he had said with a wry smile, a spark in his eyes that I realized I was missing in my own life.

Motivated by a mix of curiosity and the dull throb of midlife discontent, I made a decision that felt both thrilling and reckless. Later that day, once the house was quiet and I found a moment alone, I opened my laptop and started setting up a profile on Tinder. I hesitated momentarily before deciding to use a pseudonym and uploaded pictures that obscured my full identity, a picture of my Land Rover (plates hidden of course) completed the profile. In my profile, I described myself as an "adventurous soul seeking exciting experiences," careful to keep any detail that could link back to my real life vague.

As I clicked 'Save', I felt a rush of adrenaline. It was like stepping through a doorway into a new world, one where I could be anyone, unshackled by the expectations of my daily life. The thought was liberating and as I browsed through profiles, the possibilities seemed endless. Nairobi, with its vibrant mix of cultures and stories, was the perfect backdrop for this new adventure. I imagined discreet meetings in upscale cafes, laughter-filled evenings in hidden bars, all away from the eyes of anyone who knew me.

Each swipe on the screen was a mix of anticipation and apprehension, each match a potential gateway to the adventure I sought.

Little did I know, as I delved deeper into this digital playground, that this seemingly harmless escapade was steering me towards an encounter that would shatter the very fabric of my mundane existence.

The digital world was vast and shadowy, with paths that could lead to exhilarating highs or perilous drops. As I ventured further, drawn by the allure of the unknown, the line between my real life and my secret explorations began to blur. Unbeknownst to me, beyond the screen, eyes watched, schemes were woven, and my foray into online dating was about to intersect with a darker narrative already in motion.

CHAPTER 2:

THE DAY OF MY DEATH

I couldn't believe that this was how my life was going to end, tied up in the back of a Probox, driving along a deserted Kiambu road, with gangsters plotting how to extort my family and take all my money. Just hours ago, I had been in a hotel room about to have what I thought was the time of my life with a woman I had met on tinder. Her profile had seemed genuine, her pictures captivating, and our conversation had flowed effortlessly online. How had I missed the signs?

Nairobi's vibrant nightlife had always felt like a backdrop to my own, somewhat mundane, life. The bustling streets of Westlands, the crowded bars in Kilimani, the endless traffic snarls that could make a Toyota Vitz feel like a prison on wheels—these were the rhythms of my city. Yet, in my quest for connection, I had overlooked the dangers lurking in the shadows of those same digital spaces that felt as familiar as the streets I walked every day.

The quest for excitement, a yearning as old as time itself, finds its latest arena in the digital world. The ancient call of the wandering eye, once limited by physical and social boundaries, is now amplified, supercharged by the boundless reach of the internet and the cunning algorithms designed to exploit our deepest desires. These digital oracles, with their all-seeing eyes, craft personalized siren calls that lure us into believing in the possibility of endless new conquests. My Achilles' heel? Light skin, the undeniable allure of youth—it speaks to a primal part of me, promising to bolster my masculinity, to confirm my worth in the silent, judgmental ledger of societal norms.

But today, that very search for excitement might just be my undoing. I'm forced to see the real cost of chasing after these fleeting thrills. The qualities that once seemed irresistible to me— the fresh glow of someone young, the idea of a connection that could reignite my vitality—now feel like traps that have snared me in the most dangerous way. The algorithms, those silent matchmakers, never hinted at the risks lurking behind the profiles and pictures, where real danger hides behind attractive lies.

In my eagerness for that spark of something thrilling, I missed the shadows that stretch long and deep behind the bright screens. Hidden by the easy anonymity and infinite possibilities online, I forgot that not everyone I met had my best interests at heart. I confused carefully chosen pictures and cleverly written profiles for the reality of the person behind them, not realizing that in the vastness of the internet, there are those who prey on people like me, with motives as dark as any nightmare.

This shock, this harsh wake-up call, makes me question everything. The internet, with all its potential for connecting us, can just as easily become a place where our simplest desires turn against us, where looking for someone to share a moment with can instead bring us face to face with our own end. It shows that beneath the endless options and the lure of new encounters, our most basic needs and fears haven't changed; they've just moved onto a new stage, one that can be as dangerous as it is enticing.

As the Probox whisked past the lush coffee plantations scattered across Kiambu, the oddity of my circumstances began to deeply sink in. This wasn't merely a personal crisis; it unfolded into a grim commentary on a side of Kenyan urban life that many don't see until it ensnares them—a reality where the thrill of new connections can abruptly turn sinister, where looking for love can inadvertently invite danger. Recognizing I was neither the first nor the last to fall into such a predicament, a profound sense of despair washed over me. My life, in its final moments, seemed to unravel, leaving me to wonder about my absence's impact. Would I be remembered, or would I just vanish like a shadow at noon, leaving no mark behind?

In this moment of bleakness, my thoughts turned sharply inward. The digital personas, the endless swiping for approval, the superficial chats that I once thought brought me closer to others, now felt like hollow echoes of genuine connection. I pondered my real contributions to the world and those around me. What value had I added? What difference had my existence made? It felt as if I had been living in a mirage, my life's worth measured in likes and fleeting moments of digital attention, none of which seemed to matter now.

I thought of my family, my friends—had I been present for them, or had I allowed myself to be seduced by the allure of an online world, mistaking brief notifications for true companionship? Reflecting on this, I saw missed opportunities for real, meaningful interactions, for making memories that outlast the temporary satisfaction of online validation.

Lying there, bound in the dark, cold space of the car's trunk, the futility of my situation seemed complete. There was no grand realization, no burning desire to change or make amends. Instead, there was a resignation to the emptiness of a life that, when stripped of its digital veneer, revealed a real lack of substance.

As the vehicle hurtled through the night, my thoughts dwelled not on escape or survival but on a profound sense of regret for living a life so disconnected from what truly matters. The irony was bitter, I was searching for connection in a world that ultimately led me to this point of isolation and peril.

This wasn't just a physical journey toward an unknown, potentially grim fate, but a metaphorical descent into the realization that in the grand tapestry of life, my thread might end without having woven anything of lasting value. The grim acceptance that, perhaps, in the end, the digital chase for validation and connection had led me not to fulfillment, but to a deeper solitude, underscored the true tragedy of my tale.

CHAPTER 3:

MY TORMENTOR REVEALED

Trapped in the dimly lit, confined space of the Probox's trunk, the ride felt endless, each turn and bump a reminder of my helpless situation. It was in these desperate moments, amidst the muffled sounds of the car and my own frantic thoughts, that I first heard "The Architect" being mentioned. My captors, perhaps emboldened by their confidence in her plans and the seeming certainty of my grim fate, spoke freely in the front seats, unaware that every word filtered back to me, weaving together the pieces of the puzzle that had become my life's most dire chapter.

"The Architect has really outdone herself this time," one voice chuckled, the sound chillingly devoid of any warmth. "The guy didn't even see it coming. It's almost an art form at this point."

"Yeah, the way we reel them in with those fake profiles, it's like shooting fish in a barrel. But she's the one pulling all the strings, making sure every piece falls perfectly into place. We just do the heavy lifting," another voice replied, his tone a mix of admiration and a hint of fear.

Their casual conversation, interspersed with the occasional laughter, painted a vivid picture of The Architect's influence and the depth of her control over the operation. It wasn't just the young women on the dating apps or the enticing messages on social media; it was a whole network, a shadowy empire she commanded with precision and cruelty. Each word from my captors peeled back another layer of the sophisticated scam, revealing a chilling mix of psychological manipulation and digital deception.

I learned that The Architect's scheme was not just about luring unsuspecting victims into a trap but creating a whole narrative around it, a world so convincing that escape seemed impossible. It was a blend of reality and fabrication, tailored to exploit the vulnerabilities and desires of those caught in her web. The details of how they'd move from digital allure to physical capture, the seamless transition from an online fantasy to a real-world nightmare, unfolded as they spoke with a disarming nonchalance.

Listening to them, a cold realization washed over me. I was just the latest in a long line of those ensnared by The Architect's grand design. My role in this twisted plot was that of the victim, a character doomed from the moment I stepped into her digital maze. The confidence in my captors' voices, the ease with which they discussed their deeds, underscored a harrowing truth: in The Architect's world, I was meant to be a mere footnote, another shadow fading into the darkness of her sprawling narrative.

Their open dialogue, a mixture of boastfulness and routine, offered me a glimpse into the mind behind my capture. It painted a picture of a criminal mastermind who operated not just with impunity but with a certain dark flair, turning human vulnerability into her canvas. As the car sped through the night, the voices of my kidnappers became the unwitting narrators of my descent into the world of The Architect, a world from which escape seemed not just difficult, but futile.

My heart raced as I thought of my family, of the ransom call they would soon receive, and of the impossible choices they would be forced to make. The gang had everything they needed: my phone, unlocked; access to my social media profiles; bank details; even photos of my loved ones. I was a pawn in a game that was terrifyingly bigger than me.

CHAPTER 4:

MIRACLES STILL HAPPEN

The sudden halt of the Probox on a deserted stretch of road was the first hint of an unexpected twist in my grim saga. The silence was abruptly shattered by the sound of a heated argument outside, voices raised in a crescendo of anger and betrayal. My heart pounded against my chest; each beat a loud echo in the quiet of the night. This was my chance. With desperate determination, I worked at the ropes binding my wrists, the fibers giving way to my frantic efforts.

The night air was suddenly rent by the crack of gunshots, a terrifying symphony that seemed to freeze time itself. I held my breath, fear rooting me in place even as the ropes fell away. The gunfire ceased as quickly as it had begun, replaced by a heavy silence that seemed to weigh on my shoulders.

Gathering my courage, I clambered over into the rear passenger seats, the car eerily quiet. My heart raced as I pushed the door open, bracing myself for what I might find. The scene outside was one of chaos and carnage—bodies of the men who had taken me, now lifeless, a grim witness to their final, fatal disagreement.

Stepping out into the night, my gaze fell on a familiar shape a short distance away—my Land Rover Defender. It seemed almost surreal to see it there, a silent witness to the night's madness. I turned to the bodies lying next to the probox and quickly searched them for keys, one of them was still breathing, but at this point in time I could care less about his life after what they had put me through. The kidnappers, confident in their control over me, hadn't bothered to take the keys with them, likely leaving them in the vehicle for a quick getaway once their dark dealings were done.

My steps towards the Defender were hesitant at first, then grew more determined as the reality of my chance to escape settled in. Finding the keys in the ignition, a spark of hope ignited within me. I turned the key, and the engine roared to life, a sound that felt like a victory cry in the quiet of the night.

The engine of my Land Rover Defender roaring to life, was a clear reminder of the night's surreal turn of events. The dashboard lit up, casting an artificial glow inside the vehicle as I hurriedly put it into gear and drove away from the scene of chaos. My mind was a whirlwind of thoughts, but one immediate concern stood out: finding safety.

My phone, surprisingly overlooked by the kidnappers, was still on the wireless charging pad. Turning it on, I was greeted by the all-too-familiar home screen, with pictures of my wife and children. With a few quick taps, Google Maps was guiding me to the nearest police station, the blue line on the screen a contrast to the darkness outside.

The drive seemed endless, my mind was constantly churning, wondering if someone would show up suddenly and end my briefly found freedom, and how I had so easily been fooled by a beautiful lady. My mind drifted back to earlier in the night, trying to recall how I had found myself here.

SHADOWS BEHIND THE SCREEN - Nicholas Okumu © 2024

CHAPTER 5:

THE LAST DATE

The days leading up to that fateful evening had been a whirlwind of exhilaration. The encounters were simple, the unspoken transaction of luxury for companionship barely registering as a moral dilemma against the backdrop of my monotonous life. Yet, none of the dates had prepared me for her—*Mara*.

Allow me to describe Mara. Each prior date had served as a prelude, brief encounters that, while exhilarating, merely scratched the surface of the deep-seated yearning for excitement that had taken root within me. But there was something about Mara—her profile picture a portrait of enigmatic beauty, her eyes a gateway to a soul seemingly untouched by cynicism—that hinted this night might just breach those unexplored depths.

Her profile had been a light among the mundane, her photograph capturing a mix of exquisite beauty and an innocence that seemed almost out of place on a platform like Tinder. It was her eyes, wide and seemingly transparent, that drew me in, promising stories of a soul not yet jaded by the world.

We agreed to meet at a newly opened Amara Lounge in Kilimani, a place pulsing with the energy of Nairobi's nightlife. The locale was the newest jewel in Nairobi's vibrant nightlife, a place where the city's elite mingled with the up-and-coming, all bathed in the soft glow of opulence and the latest beats. It was the perfect backdrop for what I envisioned as a night of youthful escapade and renewed vigor.

I dressed with an eye for blending into the younger crowd, opting for a smart, slim-fit jacket that hinted at sophistication without screaming my age. A quick glance in the mirror confirmed a satisfactory concealment of the creeping grey in my hair, a nod to my vanity and perhaps a silent defiance against the relentless march of time. "Not yet old," I muttered to myself with a smirk, thinking of Larry and his less fortunate battle with baldness.

Arriving at the Lounge, I was immediately struck by the pulsating energy of the place. The air was electric, charged with the excitement and promise of nocturnal adventures. Mara was already there, seated at a corner table that offered a panoramic view of the bustling scene. Her presence dominating the dimly lit ambiance of the lounge, drawing me in with an almost gravitational pull. As she turned to greet me, her smile—a fusion of warmth and mystery—lifted the ambient light, and any lingering apprehension evaporated like morning mist under the sun. She radiated a charm that was hard to ignore, her laughter light and inviting as I approached. She turned, her smile widening in recognition, and any reservations I had about our meeting evaporated under the warmth of her greeting.

Our table became an island in the midst of the lounge's chaos. Mara laughed at my attempts at humor, her laughter genuine and infectious, and I found myself drawn into the ease of our conversation. She ordered lavishly from the menu, each dish an exploration of flavors and an ode to her zest for the finer things in life. Her appetite for life was as full as her culinary tastes, and I was all too happy to provide the feast.

As the evening wore on, our connection deepened, threading through the layers of initial attraction to something more profound. The lounge around us buzzed with life, but at our table, time seemed to slow, distilling each moment into something richer.

As the night deepened, our conversation flowed seamlessly, and the initial awkwardness gave way to a comfortable camaraderie. Emboldened by the success of the evening, I began to imagine the night extending beyond the confines of the crowded lounge, to a more intimate setting where the night could really unfold.

We got into my Land Rover, and my state of the art navigation system guided us to the Iberia Hotel in Westlands. In my mind was only the thought of the night ahead and how amazing it would be. The Iberia was far away from my usual haunts, I did not expect anyone there to recognize me. Heart pumping I booked us a room and ushered Mara in the lift to the 9th floor. There was not much of a view from our window, just an empty parking lot, illuminated by streetlights. But that was not what we had come for, I quickly closed the curtains and turned my attention back to Mara.

However, just as I was mentally preparing for the night of my life in this more private setting, a subtle shift occurred. The vibrant scene around us dimmed inexplicably, as if a shadow had passed over the sun. My head began to swim, the edges of my vision blurring as though smudged by an unseen hand. Mara's face, so vivid just moments before, wavered before me, her features dissolving into an indistinct haze.

Confusion gave way to a cold seed of dread as I struggled to grasp the rapidly unraveling reality. The sounds of the TV I had put on receded to a distant echo, and I felt myself slipping, falling through a thickening fog of consciousness. In a desperate bid to cling to reality, I reached out, trying to call for help, to anchor myself to something, anything. But my voice was lost in the void, and the world continued to fade, leaving me helplessly adrift.

In that fleeting nexus between clarity and oblivion, I realized that the night was not unfolding into an adventure, but plummeting into a nightmare. The excitement I had sought was morphing into a terror I hadn't anticipated, pulling me under into the dark undertow of consequences unforeseen and fates untold. As darkness claimed me, the last flickers of awareness sparked the chilling thought that this plunge might not just be a descent into the unknown, but a fall from which there might be no return.

Panic barely had time to register before a heavy haze dragged my consciousness down into a swirling vortex. I tried to grasp at the edges of reality, to pull myself back from the precipice that yawned suddenly beneath me, but my efforts were futile. The world slipped away in a disorienting spiral of sound and shadow, leaving me helpless in its wake.

Why was the world slipping away in a haze? Was this a medical emergency, or something far more sinister? These questions churned in the murky depths of my fading awareness, but no answers came—only darkness, deep and consuming.

In that moment, unbeknownst to me, the adventure I had so recklessly sought was spiraling into a nightmare, one that would strip away the veneer of my controlled existence and plunge me into the depths of a world I had never truly understood. The night had promised much, but as consciousness slipped from my grasp, the cost of my curiosity was about to become devastatingly clear.

CHAPTER 6:

SURVIVOR'S REMORSE

Arriving at the police station, the sight of the uniformed officers brought a sense of reality crashing back from the memories of Mara. I stepped inside, the station doors closing behind me, and approached the front desk to report what had happened.

The officers referred to me as "Mkubwa," which means "big man" or in Kenya commonly refers to a "rich/influential man" a term that felt oddly detached from the ordeal I had just survived. As I recounted the night's events, from the unexpected stop and the ensuing gunfire among the kidnappers to my eventual escape, the officers listened intently. Their expressions remained professional, yet there was a hint of something unspoken in their eyes—perhaps an understanding of the dangers lurking in the shadows of our everyday lives, or maybe they were just wondering how I survived or if I was drunk and narrating a scene from an action movie I had recently watched. Even for me as I told the story, it felt a bit out of this world, made up.

"You're lucky to be alive, Mkubwa," one officer commented after I finished my story. The statement wasn't comforting; it was a simple fact, an acknowledgment of the razor-thin margin between life and death I had narrowly escaped.

As they took my statement, the formalities of the process felt surreal, almost mechanical. There was no sense of triumph, no feeling of having overcome insurmountable odds—just the reality of survival and the bureaucratic process that followed such incidents.

After recording my statement, the decision to return to the scene felt like stepping back into a different chapter of my life, one I wasn't sure I was ready to revisit. Yet, as we drove, the early morning light began to softly illuminate the landscape, revealing the peaceful green fields of Kiambu. The beauty of the dawn made the previous night's terror feel almost like a distant nightmare, an unreal horror that couldn't possibly belong to this serene setting.

The term "Mkubwa" echoed in my mind as I left the station, the early morning light doing little to dispel the darkness of the night's events. The ordeal was over, but it left a lingering shadow, a

43

reminder of the unpredictability of life and the impersonal nature of the world we navigate.

The vehicle's quiet journey along the road contrasted sharply with the tumult of my thoughts. Approaching the area, the scenery, now bathed in the gentle light of dawn, held a deceptive tranquility. It was hard to reconcile this calm, almost idyllic landscape with the backdrop of fear and chaos it had been mere hours ago.

Stepping out of the car, the chill of the morning air mingled with the unease that clung to me, a physical reminder of the night's ordeal. The police began their meticulous search, their presence a solemn reminder of the gravity of what had occurred. Observing them, I was pulled back from the brink of the surreal peace the dawn had offered, forced to confront the reality of the situation once again.

The evidence of the night's events felt oddly out of place under the watchful eye of the sun, like remnants of a storm washed up under clear skies. The fields, so tranquil in the morning light, hid the evidence of the violence they had witnessed, speaking to the duality of places we consider safe.

I found myself looking out over the fields, their beauty undiminished by the knowledge of what had transpired. This landscape, with its gentle hills and lush vistas, momentarily lifted the weight of my experience, offering a brief respite from the heaviness of the investigation.

Yet, this return to the scene didn't bring closure; it deepened the imprint of the ordeal, embedding the experience further into my psyche. It was a vivid reminder of the fragile veneer of peace and safety that can so easily be shattered. As we left, the day fully breaking, I was more acutely aware of the balance between light and dark, order and chaos, that underpins our lives.

This chapter, now a part of my story, had changed my perception of the world. The fields of Kiambu, with their concealed stories of survival, would always be a reminder of the night when the shadows behind the screen stepped into my reality.

Driving away, the familiar streets seemed different now, colored by the experience of the past few hours. The ordeal hadn't imbued me with a new sense of purpose or a dramatic realization about the human spirit; it had simply happened, a series of events that I had managed to survive. The world moved on, indifferent to the individual dramas unfolding within it.

As I drove away from the police station, the first light of dawn began to edge its way into the sky, a silent witness to the night's events. In stories like mine, the ending seems almost predestined by some mix of fate and happenstance. But the notion of rewriting my own ending now felt like a hollow ambition. There was no grand transformation awaiting me, no vow to turn my ordeal into a crusade against the dangers of the digital world. The reality was far simpler, yet infinitely more complex.

Surviving this nightmare hadn't imbued me with a newfound purpose or a desire to serve as a warning to others. If anything, the experience had stripped away any illusions of control I once harbored. Life, I had learned, was neither a story to be authored nor a lesson to be taught. It was a series of moments, each as unpredictable and uncontrollable as the last.

My return to the familiar streets of my life was not a triumphant procession but a quiet reintegration into a world that had remained oblivious to my absence. The digital landscapes that had once served as my hunting grounds for connection now appeared to me in a different light—not because I sought to crusade against their dangers, but because I had personally brushed against the dark potential they harbored.

In the days that followed, I found myself retreating from the digital world, not out of a sense of mission, but as a natural recoil from the shadows I had encountered. My interactions became more guarded, my trust harder to earn. Not because I aimed to be an example or a guiding light, but simply because the scars of my experience had altered my perception.

The story of my ordeal remained largely my own, shared with a select few who needed to know. There was no public declaration of my survival, no cautionary tale broadcasted to warn others. It was a personal chapter, a silent transformation marked not by a shift in purpose, but by a deeper understanding of the fragility and unpredictability of life.

As life moved on, I found myself seeing the world around me with a keener eye, recognizing the thin veneer that often separates the ordinary from the perilous. My story, such as it was, didn't end with a lesson learned or a message shared.

It ended with a quiet acknowledgment of the complexities of human existence, the unseen dangers that lurk behind familiar screens, and the unspoken understanding that sometimes, survival is the only story worth telling. This story unfortunately, may change very little in the world, men will still be men, there will always be something new to entice us and lead to our downfall, but maybe, just maybe one life may be changed.

CHAPTER 7:

MARCUS'S DILEMMA

In the quiet of his sprawling office, high above the bustling streets of Nairobi, Marcus sat alone, the soft rustle of rolling paper the only sound in the room. Despite his immense wealth, he still rolled his own cigarettes—a habit rooted deep in his past, back to his days as a young man in a dusty village where luxury was a foreign concept. Each cigarette was meticulously crafted, a ritual that grounded him and reminded him of the journey that had taken him from humble beginnings to the upper echelons of the criminal underworld.

Marcus was not just any operative; he was a brilliant accountant by training, equipped with an almost photographic memory. His skills had made him invaluable, allowing him to navigate and manipulate the complex financial networks that funded their operations. These abilities had not only earned him a fortune but also the rare trust of The Architect—a woman shrouded in mystery, her identity known only to a select few, Marcus included.

SHADOWS BEHIND THE SCREEN - Nicholas Okumu © 2024

As he lit his freshly rolled cigarette, the tip glowed brightly, casting a small orb of light in the darkened room. He leaned back in his chair, exhaling a stream of smoke that swirled upwards, mingling with the shadows. His mind was a whirl of numbers and scenarios, each one meticulously catalogued and retrieved as needed. Tonight, however, his thoughts were dominated by the precarious situation they found themselves in.

Marcus knew what The Architect looked like—not just her appearance but the very essence that made her who she was. He had seen her calculated coldness up close, her eyes that seemed to pierce through the facades people built around themselves. Knowing her as he did added an extra layer of danger to his current predicament. He understood the stakes better than anyone else; he knew exactly what she was capable of.

Marcus sat in the quiet of his office, the only light coming from the burning tip of his cigarette. Each drag was a brief escape from the pressures that now threatened to engulf him. He was a seasoned player in Nairobi's shadowy underbelly, a man who thrived on control and precision, yet tonight, he found himself grappling with an unexpected and unsettling failure.

His operatives, six of the best, were gone—killed in what was supposed to be a routine capture of a single man, a doctor, a complete non-entity in the world of espionage. "A nobody, not James Bond," he muttered to himself, the irony bitter on his lips. The target's escape was not just a shock; it was a slap in the face, a direct challenge to the decade of authority and fear Marcus had built under The Architect's dark wing.

The girl they had used to lure the doctor was also dead. An unwanted but necessary casualty in the brutal calculus Marcus performed daily. No loose ends—that was the rule. Yet, as effective as it was ruthless, this policy had never before cost him so dearly in human resources.

As he flicked ash into the tray, his mind raced through the fragments of information pieced together not from an official police report—which he had yet to see—but from whispers and bribes paid to his sources within the department. Corruption in Kenya's police system was a given, an advantage he had exploited time and again to keep The Architect's operations smooth and largely unscrutinized. But now, that same corruption hinted at an impending storm. Arrests were being made, his network was slowly being unraveled, and panic was beginning to set in.

Marcus leaned back, his eyes narrowing in the smoke-filled room. How had a simple doctor, a man with no training in combat or espionage, managed to dismantle a carefully planned operation and cause the death of seasoned operatives? It was a puzzle that gnawed at him, a problem that demanded a solution before it spiraled further out of control.

The stakes were higher than ever. Failure was not an option when working for The Architect. Marcus knew the fates of those who had disappointed her before—disappearances, accidents, bodies never found. His position had always seemed secure, built on years of loyalty and success, but as he contemplated the mess, he realized his survival was no longer guaranteed.

Picking up the phone, he dialed the number of his most reliable cleaner, a man as cold and efficient as the night was dark. "Listen carefully," Marcus began, his voice steady despite the turmoil within. "We have a situation. The doctor, the one who got away, needs to be found and dealt with—permanently. And make sure there's nothing left to link back to us."

As he outlined the plan, a ruthless strategy to eliminate the doctor and secure the remaining loose ends, Marcus knew this was more than just damage control. It was a desperate bid to regain The Architect's favor and ensure his own survival.

With the call ended, Marcus sat in the silence of his office, contemplating the dark road ahead. Each decision now carried the weight of life or death, not just for the doctor but for himself as well. The police might be corrupt and his sources reliable, but in this game, every shadow could be an enemy, every ally a potential betrayer.

Tonight, the streets of Nairobi would carry more than shadows; they would bear the silent, deadly footprints of a man on a mission. As Marcus stubbed out his cigarette and prepared to leave, he steeled himself for the battles ahead. In the world of shadows he inhabited, only the ruthless survived, and he was not yet ready to be a footnote in The Architect's bloody ledger.

Suddenly the silence was broken by the ringing of his phone, it was a new number, but he knew who it was, the Architect was calling. He sighed deeply and answered the phone, "Hallo"- The voice on the other side asked a question "Have you seen the latest numbers?". Pausing briefly, he weighed his words before he answered. "Yes boss, they are not good, but we have to be careful right now, there is a lot of heat on us". The silence on the line was unnerving. "I need to see you in person", came an answer, breaking the silence. The line went silent.

He quickly turned on his computer. As he clicked through the spreadsheets, the numbers underscored the dire situation. Bribes to police and informants had tripled, expenses for covering tracks and eliminating loose ends had skyrocketed, and the cost of halting operations was eating into the reserves. The network that had once smoothly funneled funds into their coffers was now a drain on their resources.

Leaning back in his chair, Marcus lit a cigarette, the smoke curling upwards like the dissipating profits of his empire. The pressure from law enforcement was unrelenting. His insiders reported increased raids and investigations, spurred on by the very public failure of the doctor's capture. Each arrest, each interrogation of his crew, tightened the noose around their operations and pushed their activities deeper into the shadows where profitability was much harder to sustain.

The room felt colder as he thought about the meeting he had scheduled with The Architect. He would have to explain why revenues were down and why, for the first time in his tenure, the survival of their network was in question. The Architect was not known for her patience or understanding when it came to financial losses, and Marcus knew that excuses were as good as signing his own death warrant.

Flicking ash into the tray, he pondered their options. Restarting the halted operations was too risky with the current police activity. They needed something low-profile yet profitable, a new venture that could operate under the radar but bring in much-needed funds. His mind raced through various illegal enterprises—cyber scams, untraceable digital theft, perhaps even diversifying into newer, darker forms of the underworld market.

His phone buzzed again, snapping him back from his thoughts. It was one of his lieutenants, reporting yet another snag in their operations. A safe house raided, more assets seized. Each piece of bad news was a reminder of the precarious edge they were now teetering on.

As the call ended, Marcus knew that drastic measures were necessary. He started drafting plans for new operations, ones that would require minimal startup costs but promised high returns. The digital shadows where they once roamed freely were now fraught with danger, but they also offered opportunities—for those willing to delve deeper into the darkness.

He drafted a report for The Architect, outlining his plans for recovery and stabilization. His tone was careful, balancing acknowledgment of the current failures with a confident outline of potential solutions. It was a delicate dance of words, designed to assuage her concerns and buy enough time to turn their fortunes around. As always, he put the information on read only hard drive and deleted the original, especially in these times, he had to be even more careful.

As Marcus prepared for the night ahead, he felt the weight of the empire on his shoulders. The night outside was dark, reflecting his mood and the murky future that lay ahead. In the world of shadows he navigated, money was both the anchor and the lifebuoy, and he was running out of time to secure it.

Stepping out of his office into the chilling night air, Marcus was resolved. The cost of the shadows was high, but he was not ready to pay with his life just yet. The next few weeks would determine whether he could steer the ship back through stormy waters or if he would sink into the depths, another casualty of The Architect's ruthless domain.

CHAPTER 8:

HIGH STAKES IN SHADOWS

Tonight, the stakes were higher than ever. It wasn't just about saving the operation—it was about saving his own life. Marcus understood that if he couldn't persuade The Architect of his plan's viability, he might not leave the meeting alive. The underworld did not forgive, and The Architect was its unforgiving queen.

As the city passed by his window, Marcus rehearsed his pitch, readying himself for the confrontation ahead. In the world where he operated, money was the lifeblood, and he was about to argue for his life's worth. The next few hours would determine whether he could restore balance to their shaken empire or if he would become another shadow swallowed by the night.

The safe house was nondescript, blending seamlessly into Nairobi's chaotic urban sprawl. Inside, however, it was fortified like a bunker, reflecting the paranoia that accompanied those at the apex of the criminal underworld. Marcus was ushered through several security checks before he reached the inner sanctum where The

Architect waited.... a severe, meticulously organized room.

The Architect, with her commanding aura, gestured for Marcus to begin as soon as he entered. He approached the air gapped computer, inserting a USB drive he carried with him. "I've prepared a comprehensive shift in our operations to more discrete, cyber-based activities," Marcus began, his voice steady despite the undercurrent of tension.

The Architect reviewed the contents silently, her expression unreadable. She navigated through the documents with practiced ease, stopping to delve deeper into the projections and strategies Marcus had laid out. After a thorough review, she paused at the risk assessment section, her eyes scanning the data and images provided.

Her gaze fell upon a photograph of the doctor— the man whose unexpected escape had precipitated this crisis. Marcus watched closely as her stoic demeanor briefly faltered, a flicker of recognition—or was it concern? —crossing her features.

"Cancel the hit on the doctor," The Architect stated abruptly, her voice carrying a finality that brooked no argument.

Marcus hesitated, caught off-guard. "Cancel, ma'am? But he's a significant risk to—"

"Cancel it," The Architect repeated firmly, cutting him off. She looked back to the screen briefly, where the photo still displayed. "That's an order. Instead, keep him under surveillance. Make sure he knows he's being watched. Issue a warning if necessary—I want him scared, not dead. At least not yet."

As Marcus processed her command, the realization dawned on him. The doctor was not just another loose end to The Architect. He represented something more, perhaps a vulnerability in her otherwise impenetrable armor.

Leaving the safe house, the implications of what he had just witnessed whirled through Marcus's mind. In his world, personal connections were vulnerabilities, and vulnerabilities were leverage. If The Architect had a personal stake in the doctor's fate, this was information that could prove invaluable. Yet, the risk of exploiting such a discovery was immense. How he chose to proceed needed careful thought, for in the shadowy game they played, every move was fraught with peril.

Marcus stepped into the cool night, his mind racing. He now had a new task—monitoring the doctor, ensuring he remained in a perpetual state of fear. This was not just a mission to preserve operational secrecy but a maneuver to manipulate emotions, to control through fear rather than force. As he drove away, the city's lights blurred past him, each one a reminder of the intricate dance of shadows in which he was now engaged.

As weeks turned into months, Marcus continued his discreet surveillance of the doctor and his cautious probing into The Architect's interest. Despite his efforts, the information he gathered was frustratingly sparse. The doctor seemed nothing more than an ordinary man living a mundane life, far removed from their world of shadows and danger. The absence of any overt connection or unusual behavior only deepened the mystery, making Marcus's task more perplexing.

He instructed his operatives to maintain their surveillance but to blend it into their routine activities to avoid drawing attention. This was not the time to push too hard or too fast. Marcus knew the dangers of overreaching. His inquiries into the network's chatter about the doctor also yielded little more than the usual rumors and misinformation that clouded the underworld's waters.

Every evening, Marcus reviewed his notes, a growing collection of observations and hearsay that seemed more like a wild goose chase than actionable intelligence. Yet, he knew better than to let his guard down. In his line of work, appearances were often deceptive, and patience could be as crucial as action.

The only solid fact was The Architect's unexpected decision to cancel the hit—a decision that remained an enigma wrapped in a riddle. Marcus speculated about possible reasons, from professional caution to personal connections, but without concrete evidence, these remained just that—speculations.

SHADOWS BEHIND THE SCREEN - Nicholas Okumu © 2024

He kept a detailed log of his efforts, coded and locked away, knowing that even this minimal information might one day prove crucial. For now, he decided to bide his time and keep watching the doctor from a distance. There was a part of him that felt like a hunter lying in wait, patient and silent, knowing that his prey might eventually reveal its secrets.

Marcus also remained acutely aware of the danger he was in. If The Architect ever suspected his deepening interest in her decisions, or if he pushed too far and too fast into areas she preferred remained off-limits, it could spell the end of his tenure—and his life. The balance between diligence and discretion became his daily dance, one he performed with the meticulous care of a tightrope walker.

Each day that passed without significant discovery weighed on him, yet it also drove him to continue, to keep looking for that one clue that might unlock everything. For now, Marcus would continue to operate in the background, his eyes and ears open, always watching, always waiting. In the murky depths of their clandestine world, sometimes the most powerful revelations came from the quietest whispers.

CHAPTER 9:

A FRAGILE RESPITE

In the immediate aftermath of my escape, life seemed to settle into a deceptive calm. The harrowing events that had unfolded were like a distant storm, the echoes of thunder barely audible yet ominously persistent. As days turned into weeks, I found myself walking the familiar streets of Nairobi, each step heavy with a newfound caution. The vibrant life of the city, which had once imbued me with energy, now seemed laden with potential threats.

The police were reassuring, promising vigilant efforts to dismantle The Architect's network. They painted a picture of strategic raids and ongoing investigations designed to penetrate her digital veil. Yet, despite their assurances, updates were sparse, and progress seemed frustratingly out of reach. The lack of tangible results began to chip away at the initial relief I had felt, replaced by a slow-brewing realization of my vulnerability.

During this period of uneasy tranquility, I grappled with the psychological remnants of my ordeal. Sleep was fleeting, often interrupted by vivid nightmares where I relived my capture. By day, digital shadows haunted me—every email notification, every unexpected phone call sent a jolt of fear through me. It became clear that returning to my old life was not an option; the digital world I had once navigated with such carefree abandon was now a minefield.

I could feel her presence in the shadows of my daily routine, a ghostly reminder of the network that had once ensnared me. My online interactions became sources of anxiety; each ping from my phone, each unexpected email felt like it could be a trap. Paranoia crept into my sleep, tainting my dreams with visions of capture and confinement.

The feeling of being watched was incessant. It gnawed at me, eroding what little peace I managed to find during the daylight hours. I tried to tell myself it was just the aftermath, a natural response to trauma. Yet, the digital fingerprints left behind by The Architect were indelible, etched into my psyche, turning every digital shadow into a potential threat.

With the police seemingly making little headway, I started taking my own precautions. I changed passwords, enhanced security measures, and cut down on my digital footprint. Yet, each step taken to secure my privacy felt like an admission of vulnerability, an acknowledgment of the ongoing danger that lurked just beyond my screen.

My interactions became calculated, each new connection vetted with an almost obsessive caution. I withdrew from social platforms, reducing my online presence to the bare minimum. But isolation did little to assuage the fear. If anything, it amplified it, each day compounding the sense that I was alone in this fight, that The Architect was just biding her time.

In an effort to understand my enemy, I scoured the internet for others who might have encountered her web. But the stories I found only deepened my despair. They weren't tales of escape but of domination and ruin. It seemed I was an outlier, one of the very few to have slipped through her grasp. This realization didn't bring relief; instead, it highlighted just how close I had come to a fate much darker.

The solitude of my struggle was crushing. The weight of the knowledge that I had escaped where so many had not brought not empowerment, but a profound sense of survivor's guilt. Why had I been spared? And for how long?

As I documented my thoughts and fears, not as a signal of warning but as a ledger of my own fractured psyche, the act of writing became both a refuge and a reminder of my fragility. Each word I wrote was a whisper in the vast digital void, a void where The Architect still reigned with unseen omnipotence.

The message that broke the tenuous peace arrived on an ordinary evening, turning an ordinary moment into a spike of raw fear: "You can't hide forever." It was a simple string of words, but it carried the full weight of inevitability. It shattered any illusions of safety I had clung to, confirming my worst fears—The Architect hadn't forgotten about me. Not at all.

As the reality settled in, the walls of my apartment felt thinner, the buzz of the city outside more ominous. Sally had kicked me out after finding out what had happened – she had said she needed some space and we were going through counselling, I felt hopeful that she would take me back. I was going home to have dinner with her and the kids next weekend. It was my welcome home party, so to speak and I was grateful for the chance to fix our relationship.

But the message was clear: my respite was over, and the semblance of normalcy I had struggled to construct was just a fragile facade. With a few cold words, The Architect had reminded me that this was not just a battle I had escaped, but one that was ongoing and far from over.

Sleep became elusive that night, each sound a potential harbinger of something sinister. My mind raced with strategies and contingencies, but underneath it all was a simple, paralyzing fear. I was out of my depth, caught in a game where the rules were written by an unseen adversary who seemed to hold all the cards.

In that moment of acute vulnerability, I realized that surviving The Architect's initial trap was only the beginning. The real challenge lay ahead—not just in evading her grasp but in confronting the terror she wielded so adeptly. I was marked by my past escape, a loose end in her meticulously woven tapestry, and the target of a vendetta that was both digital and deeply personal.

As dawn broke, the first light seemed less a symbol of hope and more an illumination of the harsh landscape I now inhabited. My journey forward was uncertain, shadowed by the ever-present threat of a master manipulator who could bend the digital world to her will. The fight to reclaim my life and perhaps warn others was just beginning, but it would be waged in the shadows, where fear and resilience would have to coexist.

My fear was now justified and everything I feared was now a reality. It was a paranoia that clung to me, a shadow that seemed to stretch across every digital interaction. I was now desperately scrutinizing every message, every friend request, as if The Architect might be lurking behind them, biding her time.

In response I heightened my search for traces of the Architect's activities, I opened a new Tinder account with a fake profile, trying to lure her out, looking for some evidence that could help the police. My search for others who had faced her web of deceit intensified but was still dishearteningly fruitless. In fact, the stories I uncovered through hacked forums, encrypted message boards, and confidential sources painted a grim picture: most who fell into The Architect's network did not find their way out.

SHADOWS BEHIND THE SCREEN - Nicholas Okumu © 2024

They were scaring me even more and this did not feel useful anymore, I kept thinking that I had to stop, could I run, move somewhere else?

This realization only deepened the chill of isolation that had settled over me since my escape. I was an anomaly—a rare deviation from The Architect's usual script of control and ruin. Each account I read detailed meticulous manipulation, financial exploitation, and, in the most extreme cases, complete erasure of identities. These were not tales of escape but of caution, dire warnings from the digital echoes left behind by those who had vanished.

Then suddenly like a revelation from a higher power, I understood then that my escape was not just a stroke of luck; it was a responsibility. Armed with the knowledge of my unique position, I felt compelled to act, to use my experience to help for those unaware of the dangers lurking behind their screens.

My blog posts, social media updates, and contributions to online safety forums became my weapons in a fight against digital predators like The Architect. Each piece I wrote was crafted not just from my experience but was informed by the dark tales I had uncovered, each reinforcing the lesson of my own narrow escape.

This wasn't just about sharing my story; it was about filling a void in awareness, providing a critical perspective on the potential consequences of our digital engagements. I aimed to cultivate a culture of vigilance, to foster an environment where digital interactions were approached with the same caution as those in the physical world.

Yet, as I positioned myself as a rare survivor and advocate against digital predation, I knew that I was drawing fresh attention from The Architect. To her, my survival was a loose end, a blemish on her otherwise meticulous record. And as I would soon learn, her determination to correct such anomalies was as cold and calculated as the traps she set for her victims. The storm I had sensed brewing in the distance was drawing near, and I was at its center, both a target and a threat to her hidden empire.

The Architect might have believed her network impenetrable, her victims powerless, but I was proof that the shadows could be pushed back, that the prey could become the predator. It was a realization that brought a new sense of purpose, a determination not just to survive, but to fight back.

But the storm that was gathering on the horizon. The Architect, far from being a defeated foe, was preparing her response, a counterstrike that would challenge everything I thought I knew about the battle I was fighting. It was a chapter yet unwritten, a confrontation that would test the very limits of my newfound strength.

As the weeks once again melted into a cautious routine, I found myself glancing over my shoulder with unsettling frequency. The bustling streets of Nairobi, once a backdrop to my uneventful days, now seemed threaded with invisible lines of tension, a cityscape overlaid with the digital fingerprints of The Architect. Despite the semblance of normality, a persistent unease nestled in the back of my mind, whispering reminders of the ordeal I had narrowly escaped. It was during one such evening, as I navigated the crowded sidewalks of Westlands, that the first unmistakable sign appeared—a fleeting glimpse of my own face, reflected back at me from a stranger's phone screen.

As days passed, the signs became harder to ignore. My social media accounts sprouted inexplicable glitches, my emails were shadowed by echoes of unseen watchers, and my nights were punctured by anonymous calls that dissolved into silence. The Architect was laying her groundwork, demonstrating not just the reach of her influence but the depth of her vindictiveness.

It was clear that she wanted me to feel watched, exposed, vulnerable—trapped in an open space with invisible walls closing in. But if my ordeal had taught me anything, it was the value of seeing beyond the screen, recognizing the web of manipulation woven with ones and zeros. I had survived The Architect's trap once, by sheer luck, but now I realized that the only way to escape again was through understanding the game she thought she controlled.

Now, with her sights set directly on me, the game had changed. It was no longer about survival; it was about confrontation. If The Architect was coming for me, I needed to be ready. I began to retrace our digital skirmish, seeking patterns in her methods, vulnerabilities in her approach. The world of ones and zeros she mastered was vast, but it was not infallible.

I enlisted the help of a few trusted friends, individuals whose skills in the digital realm rivaled even The Architect's. Together, we started to build a countermeasure, a way to turn the tables and bring the fight to her doorstep. Our plan was not just to evade her grasp but to dismantle the network she believed impregnable.

As we delved deeper, uncovering layers of deceit and manipulation, the scale of The Architect's operation became apparent. She was more than a digital predator; she was a harbinger of a new age of crime, one that blurred the lines between the virtual and the real, exploiting the inherent trust we place in our digital lives.

But every system has its flaws, every empire its weaknesses. The Architect had made one critical error—underestimating the resolve of her prey. I had emerged from her digital labyrinth not as a victim, but as an adversary. And I was determined to bring her shadow empire crashing down, not just to save myself, but to protect others from the unseen dangers lurking behind their screens.

CHAPTER 10:

THE FADING SHADOWS:

Months passed with Marcus meticulously tracking the doctor, gathering bits and pieces of seemingly mundane details that told him little about why The Architect had spared the man's life. Yet, as the surveillance continued, a new layer of complexity emerged. The doctor, once a simple target, had transformed into something far more problematic for Marcus and his network.

The man they had once dismissed as a mere blip in their operations was now becoming an outspoken online activist. With a growing following, he shared his experiences and warnings about the dangers of the digital underworld, the same shadows where Marcus and his associates operated. His blog posts, insightful and increasingly pointed, were drawing unwanted attention—not only from potential victims who might heed his warnings but from law enforcement agencies that monitored such discussions for leads.

Marcus felt the change in the wind; the doctor was no longer just a loose end to be monitored—

he was a liability that was rapidly becoming a threat. The content of his blog was careful, never revealing specific details that could lead directly back to The Architect or her network, but the implications were clear enough to anyone versed in the coded language of the underworld.

Each new post added to Marcus's concerns, highlighting the delicate balance he had to maintain. On one hand, he needed to protect the operation from external threats, and on the other, he had to navigate the internal politics of his organization, where failure to address such a liability could be seen as a weakness.

In his secure office, Marcus reviewed the latest reports from his surveillance team alongside the doctor's most recent blog entries. The light from his computer screen cast harsh shadows across his thoughtful face. It was time to reassess their strategy. No longer could the doctor be merely watched; his online activities posed a direct challenge to the veil of secrecy that shielded their operations.

Marcus knew that any decision to escalate their response to the doctor's actions would need The Architect's approval. However, bringing this matter to her attention carried its own risks. It could highlight his previous decision to merely monitor the doctor as a misstep, especially now that the doctor was rallying others and shining a light into their dark corners.

He drafted a memo, outlining the situation in neutral terms, suggesting a need to "reassess the potential risks associated with the doctor's increasing online presence." He recommended a meeting to discuss possible courses of action, emphasizing the balance between aggressive countermeasures and the need to maintain operational security.

As he prepared for this critical discussion, Marcus considered all possible outcomes. His position required him to be a master of anticipation, always two steps ahead of both his allies and his adversaries. The doctor's transformation from victim to activist had added an unpredictable element to the game—one that Marcus needed to control before it spiraled beyond their reach.

He leaned back in his chair, exhaling slowly. The game was evolving, the stakes were rising, and he was in the center of it all. The doctor's next moves, The Architect's decisions, and his own actions would determine the fate of their shadow empire. Marcus was ready to play his part, knowing that in the intricate dance of power and survival, the slightest misstep could be his last.

In the cold, steel-framed office where even the air seemed filtered through layers of secrecy, Marcus prepared to meet with The Architect. The digital clock on his desk ticked away the seconds, each one a reminder of the gravity of the conversation ahead. He reviewed his notes one last time, each word carefully chosen to convey urgency without desperation—a fine line in the deadly game they played.

The Architect entered the room with her usual composed silence, a presence that filled the space with an unspoken authority. She seated herself across from Marcus, her eyes sharp, piercing through the dim lighting.

"Marcus," she began, her voice as measured as ever, "you asked for this meeting. I assume it's important."

Marcus nodded, clearing his throat slightly. "It is. It's about the doctor—his online activities are becoming a significant liability. He's rallying people, drawing attention to the shadows where we operate. If we don't act, it could expose more than just this operation."

The Architect listened, her expression unreadable. When Marcus finished, she leaned back, steepling her fingers thoughtfully.

"And your recommendation?" she inquired, her tone neutral.

"We need to reconsider our strategy regarding him," Marcus replied, trying to gauge her reaction. "Continued surveillance isn't enough. His influence is growing, and with it, the risks."

There was a pause, heavy with unspoken thoughts. Finally, The Architect spoke, "I understand your concerns, Marcus, but I will not escalate our actions against him. Continue your surveillance, keep him under watch. And make sure he knows he's being watched—warn him if necessary. I want him scared, but unharmed."

Marcus felt a surge of frustration, tempered only by years of discipline. "With all due respect, he's no longer just a loose end. He's a threat," he pressed, the urgency clear in his voice.

The Architect fixed Marcus with a steady gaze. "I appreciate your diligence, Marcus, but my decision stands. We do not need further complications. Your job is to manage the situation as I've instructed."

The finality in her voice left no room for further argument. As she stood to leave, Marcus caught a slight, almost imperceptible softening in her eyes. It was the first and only sign of personal investment he had ever seen from her concerning any of their marks. It confirmed his suspicions—there was something different about this case, something personal for The Architect.

After she left, Marcus sat alone in the quiet aftermath, his mind racing. Her usual ruthlessness had given way to an uncharacteristic leniency towards the doctor. What was the connection? Why the mercy? These questions gnawed at him, each one echoing louder in the silence of his office.

Determined more than ever, Marcus knew what he had to do. If The Architect wouldn't act, he would take it upon himself to unearth the secrets she wasn't sharing. Whatever the connection between her and the doctor, discovering it could shift the balance of power in his favor—or it could be his undoing.

But first, he needed more information. He decided to start where he had the most control: the surveillance team. "Increase the surveillance," he instructed his team. "Document everything. And pay special attention to anyone he meets, anyone he talks to. There's something we're missing, and I intend to find out what it is."

As Marcus set his plan into motion, the pieces of a larger puzzle began to slowly assemble themselves in his mind. Each piece was a step closer to the truth, a truth that Marcus sensed would change everything. For better or worse, he was committed to following this path, wherever it led, driven by the need to know and the instinct to survive in the high stakes shadow game they played.

CHAPTER 11:

THE ARCHITECT'S DILEMMA

In the shadow-draped office overlooking the city's twinkling lights, The Architect stood in contemplation, her posture rigid against the vast windows. The decision to remove Marcus, a decision dictated by necessity rather than desire, weighed heavily on her mind. As skilled and loyal as he had been, his probing inquiries into areas best left unexamined threatened the fabric of secrecy she had woven so meticulously around her operations. His removal was now an unfortunate but required action.

She picked up the phone, her fingers steady yet betraying a slight tremor as she dialed the number of her most reliable cleaner. With a calm, clear voice she issued the directive, ensuring the elimination would be executed with precision, leaving no trace that could lead back to her. As she ended the call, a momentary flicker of regret passed through her—a bow to Marcus's years of service, now overshadowed by the threat he posed.

Yet, even as she solidified her resolve regarding Marcus, another concern lingered in her thoughts, a dilemma that was becoming increasingly pressing. The doctor, whose activities had begun to draw unwanted attention, was another piece on her chessboard that required careful consideration. His online crusade against the digital underworld, while noble in its intent, posed a direct risk to her empire. Marcus had been correct in his assessment—the doctor was a growing liability.

As she returned to her window, looking out over the cityscape, The Architect allowed herself a rare moment of hesitation. The doctor's unwavering commitment to exposing the digital shadows could eventually force her hand. She might have to make another difficult decision soon, one that involved personal stakes far deeper than those concerning Marcus.

She pondered the layers of complexity surrounding the doctor. There was an undeniable connection there, one that compelled her to protect him thus far, keeping him alive against the pragmatic dictates of her position. Yet, the realities of her empire allowed little room for such sentiments. If the doctor continued on his current path, the risk of keeping him alive might

83

outweigh the reasons for which she had spared him so far.

"The board is set, and the pieces are moving," she murmured to herself, the words a clear reminder of the game's ruthless nature. Each move had to be calculated with precision, with personal feelings subjugated beneath the overarching strategy that guided her actions.

The Architect knew that the time might come when she might have to act against the doctor, just as she had decided with Marcus. The decision would not be easy, but in the high stakes game of power and shadow, sentiment could not dictate action. She would watch, wait, and plan meticulously. If and when the time came, she would do what was necessary, as always, to protect the empire she ruled.

Turning from the window, The Architect steeled herself for the consequences of her decisions made this night. The path forward was perilous, but she was no stranger to danger. It was the essence of her power, the foundation of her empire, and she would uphold it, whatever the personal cost.

The layers of complexity surrounding the doctor tugged at her—the undeniable connection that defied pragmatism, her thoughts it seemed kept coming back there again and again. She needed some advice, it was time to talk to her father. But she knew even now that taking the matter to him would only make things worse. "Was she ready for what was to come", she asked herself even as she accepted that there was no more choice in the matter. Although she was indeed the architect of this empire, he was The Master and no one else in the world would understand her connection to the doctor like him, He was the only one who she could talk to freely about this issue.

As she returned to her window, looking out over the cityscape, The Architect allowed herself a rare moment of hesitation. Yet, the realities of her empire allowed little room for such sentiments.

"The board is set, and the pieces are moving," she murmured to herself, repeating the words again as if to confirm them to herself. She would watch, wait, and plan meticulously. If and when the time came, she would do what was necessary, as always, to protect the empire she ruled.

"The essence of power is control," she whispered to herself as she prepared for the next steps. "And the essence of control is knowing when to act and when to wait." Tonight, she had chosen action for Marcus and patience for the doctor, each decision shaping the future of her shadowy dominion. The path forward was lined with peril, but The Architect was no stranger to danger—it was the lifeblood of her power, the currency in which she traded, and she would wield it, whatever the personal cost.

CHAPTER 12:

DON'T BITE THE HAND THAT FEEDS YOU

I arrived home to find my father in-law the sitting room with my daughters laughing at something, as always, I could see the expensive gifts on the table, who says that "money can't buy love"? They clearly had never met my dad in-law. My daughters loved the man, I think even more I suspected, than they loved me. Sally was seated across from him, her smile as always lighting up the room. He looked up at me and nodded, he could never quite hide the disdain he had for me, I would never be enough for the great Thuku Waweru, billionaire titan who allegedly was friends with the president. We briefly sneered at each other.

"Hi hun", Sally's words finally pulled me away, "How was your day"? The simplicity of her inquiry offered a momentary reprieve as I settled into the familiar role of husband and father, shedding the weight of the day's shadows. "It was fine," I replied, managing a smile as I joined them. The evening wore on with practiced normality, dinner passing as a series of light conversations and careful avoidances of anything too substantial.

The pained conversation gave me time to reflect on the opulence in which I lived, its lavish decor a nod to the wealth and taste of the Waweru family. The living space was an exquisite blend of Victorian elegance and modern luxury, with plush velvet sofas that invited comfort yet demanded respect. Intricately carved mahogany tables were adorned with vases of fresh orchids and lilies, their fragrance subtly permeating the air. The walls, lined with rich damask wallpaper in deep burgundies and golds, showcased an array of oil paintings of regal landscapes and ancestors in solemn poses. Above, a crystal chandelier hung like a crown jewel, casting a soft, ambient glow that flickered with every gentle sway.

The dining room where we gathered was a grander reflection of the living room's themes. A massive oak dining table, polished to a mirror-like sheen, stood at the center, surrounded by high-backed chairs upholstered in the finest leather. Each place setting boasted gleaming silverware and fine bone china, resting upon silk placemats. The sideboard was a magnificent piece of craftsmanship, displaying a collection of silver serving dishes and an array of spirits in cut-glass decanters.

After dinner, as Sally ushered the girls upstairs, the weight of an impending conversation settled over the dining room. Thuku's demeanor shifted; the earlier cordiality replaced by a steely resolve. Once the sounds of the girls retreating upstairs faded, he turned his piercing gaze back to me.

"We need to talk about your recent... endeavors online," Thuku began, his voice low but carrying an edge sharp enough to slice through the post-dinner calm. His fingers tapped a rhythm of displeasure on the polished surface of the dining table, each tap a measured beat of disapproval. "These shenanigans, as you call them, they're not just folly. They're airing out dirty laundry, our dirty laundry, to a world that thrives on scandal."

Before I could respond, Sally returned, sensing the tension. She slid into her seat, her presence immediately softening the room's atmosphere, yet her eyes were troubled. Thuku didn't miss a beat, turning his scrutiny towards her.

"Sally, why do you stay with him? After everything he's done?" Thuku's voice was blunt,

SHADOWS BEHIND THE SCREEN - Nicholas Okumu © 2024

his question slicing through the pretense. "He's cheated, brought embarrassment to our name. What does he have to do for you to see him for what he is?"

Sally's face flushed, a mix of anger and embarrassment coloring her features. "Dad, it's not that simple," she said quietly, her voice a mix of defiance and resignation. "What we have is complicated. There's love there, and you don't just abandon someone because of past mistakes."

Thuku shook his head, clearly unconvinced. "Love? Is love enough to overlook the shame he's brought upon our family? Is it enough to deal with the mockery?"

I felt the sting of his words, the reminder of past failings that I had worked so hard to move beyond. "I'm trying to make things right," I interjected, my voice firm yet weary. "Not just with Sally, but with everything I'm doing. These 'shenanigans' are about making things better, about fighting corruption and deceit."

"But at what cost?" Thuku retorted. "You're dragging our family through the mud. You're risking everything we've built!"

The conversation spiraled, a maelstrom of accusations and defenses. Sally tried to mediate, but the divide was too deep, the wounds too raw. As the evening wore on, the resolution seemed increasingly elusive. I excused myself, retreating to the quiet of our bedroom, the weight of the confrontation heavy on my shoulders.

I pondered Thuku's harsh words and Sally's torn loyalties. Was my quest for transparency and justice worth the personal cost? Was I selfish for pursuing a path fraught with such peril, not just for me but for those I loved? The questions haunted the edges of my mind, unresolved and echoing with the complex ties of family, love, and duty. It was especially painful to think that the problem had actually started with me cheating on Sally. It still amazed me that even after all this, she had chosen to stay with me.

Sally's attempts to mediate were heartfelt yet futile, the gulf of misunderstanding too vast to bridge with mere words. As the night wore on, the opulence around us felt more like walls closing in, a splendid prison built of legacy and expectations, each luxury a link in the chains that bound us.

Retreating from the dining room, I felt the weight of the empire on my shoulders, the echoes of the conversation mingling with the soft patter of rain beginning to tap against the windows. The opulence of our home, usually a comfort, now felt oppressive, a gilded cage that offered no true escape from the storms within or without.

The heavy atmosphere that enveloped the dining room seemed almost to condense with the mounting tension, thickening with each pointed word exchanged. The resounding echo of the last verbal volley still hung in the air when the sharp ring of Thuku's phone sliced through the tension, a jarring but welcome interruption.

He glanced at the caller ID, his expression tightening ever so slightly before excusing himself from the table with a curt nod. "This will only take a moment," he murmured, although the urgency in his brisk steps suggested otherwise. Stepping into the grandeur of the foyer, he answered the call with a terse, "Waweru speaking."

His voice, muffled slightly by the distance, carried back to us in fragments, his tone shifting from the familial authority of a patriarch to the commanding tone of a business titan within moments. Sally and I exchanged a fleeting look, an unspoken understanding passing between us that this brief hiatus in our discussion was a small reprieve, a moment to gather our thoughts and steel ourselves for the next round of familial diplomacy.

Outside, the impending storm had begun to make good on its promise, raindrops pelting the windowpanes in a steady, rhythmic pattern that matched the tapping of my own fingers against the linen tablecloth. The gusts of wind heralded the changing tide, the night air turning crisp and electric with the storm's approach.

As Thuku concluded his call, his voice raised just enough for the words "Yes, I understand," to reach us, he beckoned to his bodyguard, who had been a silent, stoic presence just outside the main door. The man, built like the proverbial brick house, snapped to attention, his demeanor respectful yet distant.

"Get the car," Thuku commanded, his tone leaving no room for delay.

"Yes, master, right away," the bodyguard responded with a deference that bordered on reverence. His use of "The Master" struck me

SHADOWS BEHIND THE SCREEN - Nicholas Okumu © 2024

anew; it was not just a title, but a declaration of Thuku's absolute authority, a reminder of his control over those in his employ, an echo of the power he wielded not just within his home but beyond its walls.

I watched, a silent observer, as Thuku returned to us. His departure was swift; a quick, almost perfunctory kiss on Sally's forehead, a nod to me that barely masked the underlying tension, and he was gone, his figure silhouetted against the floodlights that lit the sprawling driveway.

As the sound of the car engine came to life, a sleek black sedan that glinted under the downpour, I pondered the enigma of Thuku Waweru. The man was a fortress, his public and private personas so meticulously crafted and yet so distinctly different. His employees' reverence, his family's complicated love, all painted a picture of a man who was respected and feared in equal measure.

Sally sighed softly, bringing me back from my reverie. "He's gone," she murmured, her voice a blend of relief and resignation. "For now." "But please think about what he said", were her parting words as she walked upstairs to the bedroom.

The echo of "The Master" lingered in my mind, a title that carried with it weight and expectation. Why did they revere him so? What did it signify about the man I had married into, and more importantly, what shadows did it cast over the path I was choosing to walk? These thoughts swirled in my head as the storm outside reached its crescendo, mirroring the storm within the walls of the Waweru estate, each as relentless and unforgiving as the other.

CHAPTER 13:

CONVERSATIONS IN SHADOW

The meeting took place in Runda, one of Nairobi's most affluent estates, nestled along the serene stretches of Kiambu Road. This exclusive suburb is a sanctuary for the wealthy, with sprawling properties hidden behind high perimeter walls and lush greenery that offers privacy and tranquility away from the city's incessant hustle.

The estate where the meeting was held epitomized the quiet luxury of the area. A long, winding driveway flanked by towering Jacaranda trees led to a grand mansion, its architecture a tasteful blend of modern minimalism and traditional opulence. The façade was dominated by large windows and smooth stone, reflecting the early evening light and casting the house in a warm, inviting glow.

As guests approached the residence, they were greeted by the subtle sound of a water feature— a meticulously crafted stone fountain that stood as a centerpiece in the circular driveway, its gentle burbling creating a calming atmosphere. The meticulously maintained gardens surrounding the mansion boasted a variety of indigenous and exotic plants, their colors vibrant against the backdrop of manicured lawns.

The interior of the house was equally impressive. Upon entering, visitors were welcomed into a spacious foyer illuminated by a stunning crystal chandelier that hung from a high ceiling. The floors were polished marble, and the walls were adorned with an eclectic mix of African art and classical European paintings, reflecting the sophisticated taste of the homeowner.

The meeting itself was held in a stately library located towards the back of the house. This room was a haven of old-world charm and scholarly elegance, lined with floor-to-ceiling bookshelves filled with leather-bound volumes and rare first editions. The deep mahogany paneling on the walls gave the space a warm, rich feel, and a large fireplace at one end of the room added to the ambiance, its hearth aglow with a crackling fire.

The furniture was an arrangement of classic Chesterfield sofas and wingback chairs, upholstered in dark leather and grouped around an ornate Oriental rug that lay at the center of the room. The heavy curtains drawn back from the windows offered views of a serene backyard, where the twilight cast long shadows over a perfectly trimmed hedge maze and a small, secluded garden that bloomed with nocturnal flowers.

In this secluded and opulent setting, the conversations about power, loyalty, and strategy took on a weightier, almost timeless quality, as if the decisions made within these walls would echo far beyond the manicured confines of Runda. The tranquility of the location contrasted sharply with the intense deliberations that were about to unfold, making the estate not just a backdrop but a silent witness to the unfolding drama.

The room was hushed except for the rhythmic ticking of an ancient grandfather clock, its steady pulse echoing the gravity of the conversations held within these walls. This was a sanctuary where fates were forged—a place steeped in power and secrecy. The Architect approached the imposing oak desk where The Master sat silhouetted against the dim backdrop, his presence as formidable as the legacy he guarded.

Her father's gaze lifted to meet hers as she entered. It was penetrating yet carried a paternal warmth that belied the steeliness of their dialogue. "You've news," he said, his voice both a welcome and a command.

"Yes, about Marcus," The Architect began, ensuring her tone was measured and clear. "He was getting too close, uncovering aspects of our operations that require discretion. More critically, he started digging into areas concerning the doctor—areas that could expose vulnerabilities we cannot afford. His removal was precise, leaving no trace that could lead back to us or to the intricacies he nearly unearthed."

A mix of approval and concern flickered across her father's features, the weight of the loss evident even in his composed demeanor. "Marcus was a cornerstone of our operations; his loyalty was never in question. His curiosity, however, proved too perilous. Ensure his family is cared for—generously. They must not suffer for his missteps."

"Of course," she affirmed, understanding the dual nature of her father's mandate—protect the family, maintain the fortress.

"And the doctor?" The Master shifted the topic, his voice tightening slightly with the mention.

The Architect paused, her next words pivotal. "The doctor remains a complex variable. Removing him has risks that extend beyond immediate operational threats. His public persona, coupled with his unseen connections, forms a web we've only partially untangled. His disappearance could provoke inquiries, potentially tracing back to shadows we've cast far and wide."

Her father nodded slowly, processing the layers of implication. "Your caution is prudent. How do you propose we proceed?"

"We keep him under close surveillance, neutralize any immediate threats he may pose without direct action. His indirect influence offers an equilibrium of sorts—a counterbalance that, for now, serves our broader strategy."

The Master's eyes, sharp and calculating, assessed her strategy. "Very well. Maintain the status quo but prepare contingencies. We must not be caught off guard."

"I understand. The integrity of our operations remains my utmost priority," she assured him,

SHADOWS BEHIND THE SCREEN - Nicholas Okumu © 2024

her resolve mirroring the steel in her father's tone.

"As it must be," he paused, his gaze softening marginally. "Remember, the bonds of family are our greatest strength and our potential weakness. The doctor's unwitting ties to us must not become a lever against us."

Their conversation concluded with a strategic plan of patience and vigilance. The Architect felt the weight of her father's trust and the burden of the secrets she must keep. As she left the room, the gravity of their familial duty remained with her, echoing in the solemn ticking of the clock.

Outside, the estate lay serene under the veil of night, a great contrast to the storm of strategy and survival brewing within its walls. As she drove away, it started to rain, the automatic wipers on her white Mercedes came on pushing the water from side to side, though warm inside the vehicle, with its heated seats, she still felt a chill through her spine. Not everything was under her control and that concerned her greatly.

CHAPTER 14:

SHADOWS RESURFACE

After weeks of azure skies and tranquil seas, the return to everyday life was a gentle landing for me and my girls. Our holiday—spanning the pristine beaches of the Maldives, the bustling streets of Malaysia, and the serene temples of Japan—had been a glorious escape, a four-week hiatus filled with laughter and bonding. As we unpacked, our home felt warmer, the memories of our travels a fresh coat of paint on our collective lives.

Sally seemed particularly radiant, her smiles more frequent, her laughter more genuine. I couldn't help but notice certain signs, familiar yet thrilling—a certain glow, a hint of morning queasiness—signs that hinted she might be pregnant again. I kept my observations to myself for now, cherishing the possibility.

Before our trip, I had decided to listen to Sally and tone down on my activism. Life had been too chaotic, and I needed to focus on my family, to provide a sense of normalcy and peace. The holiday had been a perfect reset, and I had resolved to keep it that way. The decision hadn't come easily.

I remembered the conversation we had one late evening, the weight of it pressing on me as heavily as the darkened sky outside. We sat in the living room, the girls already asleep upstairs. Sally, her face illuminated softly by the glow of the lamp, looked at me with a mixture of concern and weariness.

"You're always on edge," she said gently, her fingers tracing patterns on the armrest of the sofa. "Ever since the abduction, you've thrown yourself into this campaign. I understand why, but it's tearing you apart, and it's affecting us. The practice is suffering, and the girls miss you. I miss you."

I had sighed deeply, feeling the truth of her words. My once-thriving practice had seen fewer patients, my colleagues covering for my absences. The trauma of my abduction still lingered, manifesting in nightmares and sudden flashes of panic. I was consumed by the need to fight back, to expose the dark underbelly that had nearly swallowed me whole.

But in that moment, looking at Sally, I realized the cost. I was losing touch with the very things I was fighting to protect—my family, my sanity, my life. The activism had become an obsession, a way to cope with the trauma, but it was also a barrier keeping me from truly healing.

"I can't keep going like this," I admitted, my voice heavy with resignation. "I need to find a balance, to be here for you and the girls. Maybe stepping back is the right thing to do."

Sally had smiled, relief washing over her features. "Let's take a break. Go somewhere far away from all this. Just us, as a family. We need to reconnect, to remember why we're here, together."

And so, the holiday had been planned, a much-needed respite from the storm of my recent past. The decision to tone down my activism was reinforced by the calm and joy I felt during our travels. The laughter of my daughters, the quiet moments with Sally, the beauty of the places we visited—they all reminded me of what I stood to lose if I didn't find a way to balance my life.

Just as life seemed to settle into a comfortable rhythm, the unexpected rang through. The first call was from Inspector Omondi, the police officer who had been diligently following up on my abduction case. The news was a mix of breakthrough and tragedy. Marcus, a name previously unknown to me, had been ready to reveal the identity of the elusive Architect in exchange for protection. But fate had dealt a cruel hand—Marcus was killed while in police custody.

"Before his untimely death, he hinted at a store of evidence, possibly enough to crack the case wide open," Inspector Omondi explained, his voice tinged with frustration and urgency. "And there's more—we found a body that matches the description of Mara, the woman you last met before your abduction."

My heart sank. Mara—the memory of that night was a shadow I had hoped to outpace. The resurgence of these details, now more tangible and menacing, reignited my fears and fueled a resurgence of my resolve to see this through, not just for myself, but for others who might fall prey.

Before I could fully process this information, another call came in. Angela Nyerere, a renowned journalist known for her fearless exposés, was on the line. Her voice was calm but carried an intensity that demanded attention.

"I'm doing a piece on the so-called Tinder scandal, where men have mysteriously disappeared after meeting women from the app. Your story of survival and escape is unique, and I believe it could be key to unraveling this dark network," Angela proposed. "Would you be willing to share your experience? Anything you remember could help others."

The dual calls threw me into a whirlwind of emotions. The quiet post-vacation bliss was suddenly overshadowed by the dark clouds of my past ordeal. As I looked at Sally, playing with our children in the living room, a mix of determination and dread filled me. I knew that stepping back into the spotlight could jeopardize the fragile peace we had built, but staying silent might mean allowing the cycle of predation and violence to continue unabated.

With a heavy heart, I knew what I had to do. The stakes were higher than ever—not just a quest for personal closure, but a fight for justice that might save others. As I prepared to meet Angela, to revisit those harrowing memories and perhaps uncover new leads, I felt the weight of the impending challenge. It was no longer just about survival; it was about resistance and revelation.

Before I could make a decision, yet another phone call came in. It was my sister-in-law, Charlene, inviting us to a family gathering to celebrate my father-in-law's 65th birthday at his residence in Runda next weekend. The thought of a family celebration offered a welcome distraction. I decided that I would put off the interview with Angela and meeting Inspector Omondi until after the celebrations. Why dampen my mood before a party? The serious stuff could wait.

SHADOWS BEHIND THE SCREEN - Nicholas Okumu © 2024

CHAPTER 15:

A DANGEROUS TURN

Inspector Omondi was deep in paperwork when the call came through. It was late, and the dim light from his desk lamp cast long shadows across the cluttered surface. He was used to receiving strange calls at odd hours, but the urgency in the voice on the other end of the line immediately caught his attention.

"This is Marcus," the voice said, barely above a whisper. "I need your help. They're going to kill me."

Omondi straightened in his chair, the fatigue of a long day suddenly forgotten. Marcus. The name was unfamiliar. "Who are you?" he asked, his voice steady.

"I know you're the investigating officer on the doctor's case," Marcus replied hurriedly. "I have information that can help you. But you need to protect me."

"Where are you?" Omondi asked, his tone urgent.

Marcus gave him an address, a nondescript location on the outskirts of the city. "Meet me there in an hour. And come alone."

An hour later, Omondi found himself in a dimly lit alley, the air heavy with tension. Marcus emerged from the shadows, his eyes darting around nervously. "Thank you for coming," he said, his voice trembling. "I don't have much time. They're closing in on me."

Omondi led Marcus to his car, the two men speaking in hushed tones as they drove to a safe house in the Mua Hills, an isolated area far from the city. The house was modest and chosen for its seclusion, with no other structures for miles around. It was the perfect place to keep Marcus hidden. It had been specifically chosen because they could see anyone approaching from miles away.

Once inside, Omondi secured the perimeter and turned to Marcus. "You need to tell me everything," he said. "If we're going to protect you, I need to know exactly what we're dealing with."

Marcus nodded, his expression grave. "I've been part of the Architect's operations for years, but

SHADOWS BEHIND THE SCREEN - Nicholas Okumu © 2024

recently I found out things I wasn't supposed to know. They were planning to eliminate me."

He reached into his pocket and pulled out a crumpled piece of paper. "This is the location of the girl who was with the doctor when he was kidnapped," he said, handing it to Omondi. "It's a show of good faith. I know more—much more—but I need your guarantee of protection."

Omondi looked at the paper, then back at Marcus. "We'll get you an immunity deal and witness protection," he said. "I'll make the arrangements. But you need to stay here and keep your head down. No one can know where you are."

The next few days were a flurry of activity. Omondi coordinated with his superiors, setting up the paperwork for Marcus's immunity deal and arranging for witness protection in a foreign country. Every detail had to be perfect to ensure Marcus's safety.

The safe house in Mua Hills was a solitary building surrounded by rugged terrain. Its isolation was both its greatest asset and a potential vulnerability. Omondi posted trusted officers at strategic points around the property, confident that the distance from civilization would deter any threats.

But just as everything seemed to be falling into place, disaster struck. Omondi was at his desk, finalizing the last of the documents, when he received a frantic call from the officer stationed at the safe house.

"Inspector, we've got a problem. Marcus is down."

Omondi's heart raced as he sped to the safe house, the sirens of his police car blaring. When he arrived, the scene was chaotic. Officers were everywhere, and the air was thick with tension. He pushed through the crowd, his eyes falling on Marcus's lifeless body. A single bullet wound to the head. A sniper's work.

The shot had been taken from an incredible distance, attesting to the skill of the assassin. Omondi's mind raced with questions. How had they found him? Marcus's information was critical, and now it was lost.

Omondi knelt beside Marcus's body, a sense of failure washing over him. He had promised protection, and now the man who could have brought down the Architect was dead. His

SHADOWS BEHIND THE SCREEN - Nicholas Okumu © 2024

thoughts turned to the doctor, unaware of the storm that was once again brewing on the horizon.

He still had one thing, the body of the girl, maybe there was still hope of finding something useful.

The sniper received his orders through the dark web, a shadowy corner of the internet where anonymity was a currency as valuable as Bitcoin. The email was brief and to the point, containing a single directive: eliminate the target known as Marcus. Attached to the email was a photo of Marcus, his location, and detailed coordinates of a safe house in the isolated Mua Hills. The payment, a substantial sum in cryptocurrency, was already sitting in his digital wallet, awaiting confirmation of the kill.

As the sniper, known only by his alias "Phantom," read through the instructions, he felt a familiar thrill. This job was different. The distance from which the shot would have to be taken was extraordinary, bordering on the impossible for most, but Phantom was no ordinary marksman. He thrived on such challenges.

Phantom's preparation was meticulous. He chartered a private helicopter under a false name, using untraceable funds to ensure no trail led back to him. The pilot believed he was taking Phantom on an aerial tour of the area, flying him from and back to Wilson Airport in Nairobi. From the air, Phantom scoped out the Mua Hills, identifying potential vantage points that offered a clear line of sight to the safe house. He noted the terrain, the elevation, and the natural cover. After days of reconnaissance, he selected a nest site nearly two miles away—a rocky outcrop with a direct view of the target area.

Phantom returned to Nairobi with the pilot, blending seamlessly into the city's hustle. He boarded a matatu to Mua Hills, his rifle disassembled and packed into a nondescript backpack, indistinguishable from the luggage of other travelers. The journey was mundane, the contrast to the extraordinary task ahead sharp and deliberate.

The sniper's nest was carefully chosen for its isolation and elevation. The rocks provided natural concealment, and the distance ensured he would be far out of reach from any immediate threat. Setting up his equipment, Phantom worked with the precision of a surgeon. His rifle, a custom-made .50 caliber, was capable of extreme long-range shots, its barrel fitted with a high-powered scope. He calibrated the scope meticulously, accounting for wind speed, humidity, and the slight curvature of the earth over such a vast distance.

Lying prone on the rocky outcrop, Phantom scanned the safe house through his scope. The time of day was crucial; he chose late afternoon when the sun was beginning to set, casting long shadows that would further obscure his position. As he settled into his nest, the anticipation built. He had only one shot—one chance to ensure the mission's success.

Phantom waited for hours, his body perfectly still, not even moving to eat or take a bathroom break. His patience and discipline were unparalleled, a salute to his training and experience. Through the scope, he saw the activity at the safe house. Officers moved in and out, securing the perimeter. Then, he saw his target. Marcus was standing by a window, speaking animatedly with an officer. Phantom's breathing slowed, his heart rate dropping as he entered the calm state of focus that preceded every shot. He adjusted for the slightest movement, his finger hovering over the trigger.

In that moment, everything seemed to slow. Phantom squeezed the trigger gently, feeling the rifle's recoil as the bullet sped towards its target. It was a shot few could make, traversing an incredible distance with pinpoint accuracy. The bullet shattered the window and struck Marcus in the head, dropping him instantly.

Phantom watched through the scope as chaos erupted at the safe house. He didn't linger to admire his work. Efficiency was key. He disassembled his rifle, packed up his gear, and began the long walk back to the main road, where he would catch another matatu back to Nairobi. The journey was uneventful, his presence unnoticed among the throng of daily commuters.

As Phantom blended back into the city's anonymity, his mind was already on his next steps. The transaction was complete. The cryptocurrency payment, now confirmed, would be laundered through various digital channels, ensuring it was clean by the time it reached his usable accounts.

By the time law enforcement began piecing together what had happened, Phantom was miles away, another ghostly trace in the annals of covert operations. The job had been executed flawlessly, leaving no evidence behind. To the world, Marcus's death was a mystery—a demonstration of the sniper's deadly efficiency.

As Phantom navigated the crowded streets of Nairobi, he felt a rare moment of satisfaction. The impossible shot had been made, and he had once again proven why he was the best. The world would move on, oblivious to the shadows in which he operated, leaving only the ripples of his actions behind. But he also remembered that one client, whose hit had been cancelled at the last minute, he had still been paid in full. That guy did not know how lucky he was, or how good Phantom was. He also remembered his last kill, a girl struggling for breath as he choked her with a garrot, he remembered the surprise on her face, as they had just gone on a lovely date and spent a fantastic night together. Phantom smiled; he had other skills too.

CHAPTER 16:

UNEARTHING SECRETS, CHASING GHOSTS

Inspector Omondi stood at the edge of the coffee farm, his eyes scanning the expanse of green that stretched out before him. The sun was just beginning to rise, casting a soft glow over the landscape. The air was crisp and filled with the earthy scent of wet soil and coffee berries. It was hard to believe that such a serene place could be the site of something so sinister.

The call had come early that morning, notifying him that they had finally received the go-ahead for the exhumation. The location had been provided by Marcus before his untimely death—a piece of crucial information that might just break the case open.

The site was near Tatu City, along the road from Kiganjo, just after the T-junction from the road coming from Ruiru town, near NIBS College. As Omondi approached, he could see the team of forensic experts and officers already at work, the area cordoned off with bright yellow tape that sharply contrasted with the surrounding greenery.

Dr. Kibet, the lead pathologist, greeted Omondi with a nod. "Inspector, we're ready to begin."

Omondi nodded, feeling the weight of the moment. "Let's get started."

The forensic team moved with practiced efficiency, carefully digging into the ground. The atmosphere was tense, each shovel of dirt bringing them closer to the truth buried beneath. After what felt like an eternity, the dull thud of a shovel hitting something solid broke the silence.

Slowly, reverently, the team uncovered the remains. The body was in a state of advanced decomposition, the months since her death having taken their toll. The smell was overpowering, but the team worked diligently, unfazed by the grisly task.

Omondi's eyes were drawn to the small piece of paper clutched in the corpse's hand. It was a curious detail, something that seemed out of place in the grim scene. Carefully, Dr. Kibet extracted the paper, handing it to Omondi with gloved hands.

Unfolding it gently, Omondi saw that it was a receipt from a small, nondescript café. The date on the receipt was the same day the doctor had gone on his ill-fated date with Mara. His mind raced with possibilities—why had she been holding onto this? What significance did it have?

"We'll need to analyze this," Omondi said, handing the paper to one of the forensic experts.

Dr. Kibet continued his examination of the body. "Initial observation suggests strangulation," he said, his voice clinical yet respectful. "But I'll need to conduct a full examination back at the lab to confirm the cause of death and look for any other signs of foul play."

Omondi nodded, his mind already spinning with questions. The piece of paper could be a clue, or it could be a red herring. Either way, it was something to follow up on. As they carefully transported the remains, Omondi couldn't shake the feeling that they were on the brink of something significant.

The journey back to the lab was somber, the weight of the investigation heavy in the air. Omondi thought about Marcus, the doctor, and the intricate web of deception they were trying to untangle. Each piece of evidence was a thread that could either unravel the mystery or tighten the noose around those responsible.

At the lab, Dr. Kibet got to work immediately, his team setting up for a detailed examination. Omondi watched through the observation window, his mind running through the steps they needed to take next. The receipt would be analyzed, cross-checked with any known locations frequented by the suspects, and hopefully provide a lead.

As the hours passed, Omondi felt a mixture of hope and frustration. The exhumation had provided them with new information, but it also raised more questions. Who had killed Mara? Why was she holding onto that receipt? And how did it all connect to the doctor and the elusive Architect?

Deep in thought, Omondi was jolted back to reality as Dr. Kibet emerged from the examination room. "Inspector," he said, "we've found something else."

Omondi's heart skipped a beat. "What is it?"

Dr. Kibet held up a small, blood-stained necklace. "This was found around her neck, hidden under the layers of decomposition. It could be significant."

Omondi took the necklace, examining it closely. It was a simple piece, but the bloodstains suggested it had been part of the struggle that ended Mara's life. "Thank you, Doctor. This could be the breakthrough we need."

As he left the lab, Omondi's resolve hardened. They were getting closer, inch by inch, to uncovering the truth. The path ahead was still murky, but with each new piece of evidence, the fog was beginning to clear. The Architect's web was vast and intricate, but Omondi was determined to bring it down, no matter the cost.

With the receipt and the necklace now key pieces of evidence, Omondi knew their next steps would be crucial. The journey to justice for Mara, Marcus, and all the others affected by the Architect's machinations was far from over, but Omondi felt a renewed sense of purpose. They were on the right track, and nothing would deter him from seeing it through to the end.

The next morning, Inspector Omondi arrived at the precinct, determined to piece together the new leads from the exhumation. He had spent most of the night reviewing the evidence, making sure everything was documented and secured. But as he entered the evidence room, he was greeted by an eerie silence and a sense of foreboding.

The room was in disarray. The secure storage where the body of Mara and the collected evidence had been kept was wide open. Omondi's heart sank. He rushed to the lockers and found them empty—everything was gone. The body, the photographs of the necklace, the receipt—everything.

"How the hell...?" Omondi muttered under his breath, his mind racing. He turned to the officers nearby, who looked equally shocked and confused.

"We checked the security footage, sir," one of the officers reported, his voice trembling slightly. "There's nothing. It's like whoever did this knew exactly where the cameras were. They didn't leave a trace."

Omondi's thoughts were a whirlwind. Who could have pulled this off? Stealing a body from the morgue and erasing all traces of evidence wasn't something just anyone could do. This required

SHADOWS BEHIND THE SCREEN - Nicholas Okumu © 2024

resources, connections, and a level of audacity that was deeply unsettling.

He pulled out his phone, desperately hoping that the photos he had taken of the receipt were still there. As he unlocked the device, the screen flickered and then went black. A message flashed briefly: "Data corrupted." It was a virus, and a sophisticated one at that. His last hope of salvaging any information vanished before his eyes.

"Damn it!" Omondi cursed, slamming his fist on the table. He felt a mixture of frustration and helplessness. How could they be so thoroughly outmaneuvered?

As he tried to gather his thoughts, an officer approached him with a small, plain package. "This just arrived for you, sir."

Omondi took the package, a sense of dread washing over him. He carefully unwrapped it, revealing a single bullet nestled inside. There was no note, but the message was clear. This was a warning.

His mind raced. The implications were chilling. Whoever was behind this had the reach and the power to infiltrate secure facilities and eliminate evidence without leaving a trace. They could plant viruses and send ominous threats without fear of repercussions.

Omondi sat down, the weight of the situation pressing down on him. He was at a crossroads. Pursuing this case meant putting his life on the line. The bullet was a grim reminder of the dangers that lay ahead.

As he stared at the bullet, doubts began to creep in. Was this worth the risk? He thought about his family, the life he had built, and the future he could lose. The cost of pursuing the case seemed insurmountable.

The decision gnawed at him. He had dedicated his life to justice, but this was different. The enemy was invisible, powerful, and seemingly omnipresent. Walking away meant safety but at the expense of his principles. Continuing meant danger, possibly death, but with the hope of uncovering the truth.

His phone buzzed with a text from a colleague. "Any updates?" it read. How was it working now? Omondi stared at the screen, the gravity of his choice pressing down harder. Could he really put everything on the line for this?

As the seconds ticked by, he felt the pull of duty battling against the instinct for self-preservation. The bullet on his desk was more than a warning—it was a question, one that demanded an answer.

Finally, with a deep breath, Omondi made his decision. He would tread carefully, reevaluate his strategy, and consider all options. But one thing was clear: the case wasn't closed, not yet. He would find a way to continue, but he would do it on his terms, with a new level of caution and cunning.

CHAPTER 17:

FAMILY REVELATIONS

The house in Runda, as grand as ever, stood resplendent under the late afternoon sun. The long, winding driveway flanked by towering Jacaranda trees led guests to the mansion where the party was in full swing. The gentle sound of the stone fountain in the circular driveway added to the festive atmosphere, while the meticulously maintained gardens showcased vibrant blooms against a backdrop of manicured lawns.

Inside, the spacious foyer was alive with the sound of laughter and conversation. The crystal chandelier sparkled, casting a warm glow over the guests as they mingled. The dining room, with its massive oak table and gleaming silverware, was set for the cake-cutting ceremony. Guests moved between the rooms, admiring the eclectic mix of African art and classical European paintings adorning the walls.

I observed the grandeur around me, feeling a twinge of unease. Despite the opulence, the house felt like a gilded cage, with secrets lurking in its shadows. Sally, radiant as ever, flitted from guest to guest, her smile lighting up the room. Charlene, poised and elegant, stood near their father, Thuku Waweru, who commanded the room with his presence.

As the cake-cutting session approached, Thuku called for attention. The guests gathered around, the anticipation palpable. The Master, as everyone reverently called him, began his speech.

"Thank you all for being here to celebrate my 65th birthday," Thuku began, his voice resonating with authority and warmth. "I am blessed to have a family that has stood by me through thick and thin. Today, I want to acknowledge my two daughters, Sally and Charlene, who have been more than sons to me."

I felt a surge of pride as Thuku praised Sally. "Sally has done a sterling job running the businesses we own," Thuku continued, his eyes shining with pride. "Her dedication and hard work have been the backbone of our success."

Then Thuku turned his gaze to Charlene. "And Charlene, well, she is the architect of all our success, both literally and figuratively," he said with a smile. "Her brilliance and vision have taken us to heights we could only dream of."

The word "architect" jolted me. I looked at Charlene, who met my gaze with an inscrutable expression. The realization began to dawn on me. Could Charlene be the Architect I had heard about? The one Marcus had mentioned?

As Thuku continued his speech, my mind raced. Why had I escaped the thugs that day when almost no one else did? Why had I been kept alive when others were systematically eliminated? I glanced around the room, suddenly feeling out of place among people I barely knew. Despite being part of the family for years, I realized how little I knew about my in-laws and their mysterious business empire.

After the cake was cut and the toasts made, I found myself standing alone, lost in thought. I remembered how everyone who worked for Thuku referred to him as "The Master" instead of "Sir." I had always found it peculiar but had never given it much thought. Now, the pieces were beginning to fit together, forming a picture I wasn't sure I wanted to see.

Sally, noticing my pensive mood, joined me. "You okay?" she asked, concern evident in her eyes.

"Yeah, just thinking," I replied, forcing a smile. "Your father's speech got me thinking about a lot of things."

She nodded, understanding. "He has a way of doing that. But tonight is about celebration. Let's try to enjoy it."

I nodded, but my mind was already elsewhere. The evening wore on, and my curiosity grew. I wanted to find out more about my father-in-law's empire, about the true nature of their business, and about Charlene's role in it all. But this wasn't the time or place. I would have to wait, bide my time, and dig deeper when the moment was right.

But another thought crossed my mind about how ridiculous all this sounded. I imagined myself telling it to Inspector Omondi and all I could visualize was how he would burst out laughing and tell me that I was crazy. With that I put the matter to rest, at least for the moment, we were at a party after all, right! I even imagined Sally being part of a crime family and just grinned like an idiot; "you are getting too paranoid", I told myself as I grabbed a drink from the passing waiter's tray.

As we left the party, I felt a mix of emotions—curiosity, apprehension, and a gnawing sense of unease. The more I thought about it, the more I realized that my life was intricately intertwined with secrets and dangers I had never imagined. And as I drove away from the grand estate, I knew that finding the truth would always be my next mission, no matter the cost.

CHAPTER 18:

THE OTHER SIDE OF THE MIRROR

Charlene watched her brother-in-law Andrew mingle with the guests, a scowl threatening to break through her composed exterior. He was only alive because Sally loved him, and they had children together. She thought back to that fateful day of his abduction, how she had sent Phantom to rescue him, taking care of six of her best men in the process. The investigation by the police had almost destroyed their business, forcing her to sacrifice Marcus, a trusted lieutenant, just to keep this useless man a secret. She wished him dead already.

Her disdain for Andrew threatened to show on her face, so she kept a low profile during the party, avoiding prolonged conversations. She moved through the opulent rooms, each corner of the mansion a reflection of their wealth and power. But beneath the polished marble floors and the glittering chandeliers lay a network of secrets, and Charlene was the architect of it all.

As the cake-cutting ceremony approached, Charlene stayed in the background, watching Thuku command the room. His speech was warm and filled with praise, but she knew he had a tendency to reveal too much when tipsy. Her father's words were intended to celebrate, but they also hinted at the family's hidden truths.

"And Charlene, well, she is the architect of all our success, both literally and figuratively," he said, his voice carrying a hint of pride and a deeper meaning only a few would understand. Charlene saw Andrew's startled expression and knew he was beginning to piece things together.

She maintained her composure, but inside she was seething. The complications her brother-in-law brought were becoming too great a risk. She thought about the lengths she had gone to protect their secrets, including orchestrating the theft of Mara's body from police custody.

Sally had no idea that their family, in addition to running legitimate businesses, was also a large crime syndicate. Their father had long ago decided to protect Sally from the darker side of their operations. As the last born, he loved her too much to let her be tainted by their criminal activities. Sally had gone to the best schools, including Wharton Business School, and inherited what on the surface was a legitimate business empire. She didn't know it was all a front to launder their family's ill-gotten wealth.

As the evening wore on, Charlene mingled with the guests, her mind constantly returning to the problem that was her brother-in-law. Perhaps the time had come to end his life and leave Sally a widow. She had dealt with more challenging obstacles in the past, and this was no different.

As the party drew to a close, Charlene kept a close watch on Andrew. She saw him leave with Sally, their departure marked by a shared look of concern and curiosity. The pieces were moving on the board, and Charlene knew she had to stay several steps ahead.

Driving away from the estate, Charlene's thoughts were a mix of determination and apprehension. She had to ensure the integrity of their empire, even if it meant making difficult decisions. The gilded cage of their wealth and power had its price, and Charlene was prepared to pay it to protect their legacy.

CHAPTER 19:

VANISHING TRAILS

I decided to call Inspector Omondi for an update before meeting the reporter. The phone rang for what felt like an eternity before he answered.

"Omondi speaking."

"Inspector, it's Andrew. Do you have any updates on the case?" I asked, trying to keep the anxiety out of my voice.

There was a pause on the other end before Omondi sighed. "I'm afraid I have some bad news. All the evidence we collected, including the photographs, is gone. Stolen overnight from evidence and the city mortuary."

I was stunned. "How is that possible? Who could do something like that?"

"That's what I'm trying to figure out," Omondi replied, frustration evident in his tone. "But it seems whoever is behind this has resources and connections we can't match. Even the victim's body disappeared without a trace, from the largest mortuary in the country!"

I thought about my suspicions based on what I had observed at the party, but without concrete evidence, it would sound like paranoia. "What happens now?" I asked instead.

Omondi hesitated. "With no evidence, I have no choice but to drop the case officially".

He went silent for what seemed to be a long time before adding, "I'm also seeking a transfer to Kisumu to be closer to my family. I'm sorry, Dr. Andrew. I wish you all the best."

The line went dead, leaving me feeling abandoned and vulnerable. The weight of Omondi's departure was heavy. It felt like the final nail in the coffin of any hope I had for justice.

Desperation set in as I dialed the reporter's number. Angela Nyerere had been my last hope, but she didn't answer. Days passed, and my calls went unanswered. Worry gnawed at me. Then, on the seventh day, as I watched the evening news, my worst fears were confirmed.

"Breaking news: Renowned journalist Angela Nyerere was found dead in her home this morning. No evidence of foul play has been found. Her housekeeper discovered her body after returning from leave. She appears to have died peacefully in her sleep."

The words echoed in my mind, disbelief and dread mingling. Peacefully in her sleep? It was too convenient. I knew this was the Architect's doing, another clean-up to eliminate a threat.

My thoughts spiraled. The Architect would go to any length to keep their secrets, eliminating anyone who posed a risk. I thought about my family, Sally, and our daughters. Could I afford to keep pursuing this, knowing the danger it posed to them?

I was left pondering my options. The fight seemed unwinnable; the cost too high. Maybe it was time to let this go, to retreat into the semblance of a normal life and protect what truly mattered. As I sat in the silence of my study, the shadows seemed to close in, the weight of my decision pressing down on me.

I had not come to this fight willingly but through an unwitting mistake. From whatever information I could gather it seemed that my enemies were within my family, they had chosen to let me live, but also shown me that thy would go to any lengths necessary to keep me quiet. I was not seeing too many other options left for me.

CHAPTER 20:

THE ARCHITECT'S LAST LAUGH

Charlene sat in her luxurious office; the expanse of Nairobi's skyline visible through the floor-to-ceiling windows. The soft hum of the air conditioning was the only sound as she leaned back in her leather chair, a satisfied smile playing on her lips. The events of the past few months had tested her mettle, but now, she could finally revel in the triumph.

The investigations that had once threatened to unravel everything had been effectively silenced. Inspector Omondi's transfer to Kisumu had been a masterstroke, ensuring that the one man with the tenacity to pursue the case was now miles away, preoccupied with his own family matters. The stolen evidence and the death of Angela Nyerere had sent a clear message: The Architect was untouchable.

Business was booming once again. The disruptions caused by Marcus's betrayal and the police scrutiny had been mere bumps in the road. New blood had been brought in to replace Marcus, and the organization was running more smoothly than ever. These new recruits were loyal, efficient, and most importantly, completely unaware of the internal power struggles that had led to their predecessor's downfall.

Charlene allowed herself a moment to think about Andrew. Her useless brother-in-law had finally toned down his crusading ways. The family holiday had done wonders, and he seemed content to return to his medical practice and focus on his family. He was no longer a threat, merely a pawn in a game he didn't even realize was being played around him.

She considered the irony of it all. Andrew, the man who had come so close to exposing her, was now blissfully ignorant of the empire that thrived in the shadows. It amused her to think how he had no idea that his life was spared only because of Sally's love for him. She had sent Phantom to rescue him on the day of his abduction, sacrificing six of her best men to maintain the secret. It had been a calculated risk, but one that had paid off handsomely.

Her thoughts turned to her father, Thuku Waweru, the Master. She felt a surge of pride thinking about him. She owed her success to his teachings and his unwavering belief in her capabilities. Despite the gravity of their operations, she had always felt a sense of security knowing he was there, a guiding force behind her every move. The upcoming visit to him would be a chance to bask in his praise, to celebrate their continued dominance.

Charlene glanced at the clock. It was time to leave for another meeting, another piece of the intricate puzzle that was her life. As she gathered her things, she paused to look at the photograph on her desk. It was a picture of her and Sally, taken years ago at a family gathering. Sally, blissfully unaware of the darker side of their family empire, had always been the golden child. It was better that way. Charlene had taken on the burden of their family's secrets, protecting Sally from the harsh truths.

With a final glance at the skyline, Charlene walked out of her office, her heels clicking with purpose on the marble floor. The Architect had won this round, and the future looked brighter than ever. The last laugh was hers, for now, and she intended to savor every moment of it.

CHAPTER 21:

THE HUNTER IN SHADOWS

Inspector Omondi felt the weight of his new responsibilities as he entered the nondescript building in Runda. From the outside, it appeared to be just another affluent property in this wealthy suburb, but inside, it housed the nerve center of a covert operation that aimed to dismantle one of the most powerful cartels in Kenya.

His brief stint in Kisumu had been a ruse, a calculated move to throw off anyone who might suspect his true intentions. In reality, Omondi had been promoted and tasked with leading a special task force dedicated to investigating the elusive network that had orchestrated so many high-profile crimes. The words on the lost receipt had been a crucial lead, and with Interpol's help, he had tracked the money trail to this very property in Runda.

The revelation that the estate belonged to Thuku Waweru, the doctor's father-in-law, had been a shock. However, their target was not Thuku Waweru himself, but a member of his security team who went by the alias "Buff". As of now

SHADOWS BEHIND THE SCREEN - Nicholas Okumu © 2024

they had no evidence that Thuku Waweru himself had any connection to the case. Omondi now questioned everything he thought he knew about Andrew. Had he been too trusting? Was Andrew a mole, a pawn used to feed him just enough information to mislead his investigation?

As he walked through the building, Omondi replayed the events that had led to this moment. The case had seemed to fall apart inexplicably, with key pieces of evidence disappearing and potential witnesses turning up dead. How else could the cartel have known about Marcus and the body they had retrieved? The realization that Andrew might have been compromised gnawed at him, but he couldn't let that cloud his judgment.

Inside the command center, his team of three operatives—each handpicked for their expertise and loyalty—were already monitoring the estate's activities. The room was filled with state-of-the-art surveillance equipment, from high-resolution cameras to sophisticated listening devices. Every conversation, every movement within the estate was being recorded and analyzed in real-time.

SHADOWS BEHIND THE SCREEN - Nicholas Okumu © 2024

"Status report," Omondi ordered, his voice steady but firm.

One of his operatives, a tech specialist named Kamau, glanced up from his monitors. "Everything is quiet for now. We've intercepted some communications, but nothing that directly implicates Waweru. They're careful."

"They always are," Omondi muttered. "But everyone makes a mistake eventually. And when they do, we'll be ready."

He had deliberately compartmentalized the operation, ensuring that only he had the complete picture. This way, if any one of them were compromised, the integrity of the investigation would remain intact. Trust was a luxury he could no longer afford. Knowledge of this surveillance operation was on a need-to-know basis, and right now, only his immediate team knew of its existence.

Omondi settled into his chair, eyes fixed on the screens that displayed various angles of the estate. They had a long road ahead, but he was patient. This was a game of shadows and subtlety, where the slightest slip could tip the balance.

SHADOWS BEHIND THE SCREEN - Nicholas Okumu © 2024

As he watched, he couldn't help but think about Andrew. If the doctor was innocent, he had unwittingly been a part of a much larger, more dangerous game. If he was complicit, then Omondi would see to it that he faced justice along with the rest of them.

For now, they would wait and watch, blending into the shadows that cloaked their prey. Omondi knew that the facade of tranquility would eventually crack, and when it did, he would be there, ready to strike. This time, he would not be misled. The hunt had just begun, and the hunter was prepared to play the long game.

Patience was his ally, and vigilance his weapon. In the depths of Runda, where wealth masked corruption, Omondi and his team remained the unseen guardians, silently waiting for the moment when they could bring the darkness into the light.

EPILOGUE:

THE ARCHITECT'S LAST LAUGH, OR NOT

Charlene Waweru, known in the shadows as The Architect, sat in her opulent office, reflecting on the tumultuous events of the past few months. Business was booming once again, and the investigations that had threatened her empire had been deftly silenced. The death of Marcus, while unfortunate, had been a necessary move. She had replaced him with fresh blood—loyal, ambitious, and untainted by the past.

As she looked out over the sprawling cityscape, a rare smile touched her lips. Her brother-in-law, Andrew, seemed to have settled down from his crusading ways. The threat he once posed had been neutralized, and he now appeared to be focusing on his family. His recent vacation with Sally and the kids had done wonders. Charlene almost felt a pang of guilt—but only almost. In this game, feelings were a luxury she couldn't afford.

She considered visiting her father soon, to bask in the glow of his praise. He had always seen her as the true architect of their success, a title she had earned through years of meticulous planning and ruthless execution. As she pondered the future, a thought nagged at her—was it really over?

Inspector Omondi entered the nondescript building in Runda with a sense of renewed purpose. The quiet suburban tranquility masked the intense operations within. His transfer to Kisumu had been a ruse, a cover for his promotion to lead a special task force investigating the powerful cartel that had eluded justice for too long.

He remembered the words on the receipt Marcus had mentioned before his untimely death. Tracking it had led Omondi to Phantom, the elusive assassin. Though they hadn't caught him, they had traced the funds to the owner of this property in Runda—Thuku Waweru, Andrew's father-in-law.

Omondi's trust in Andrew now seemed questionable. How had they known about Marcus and the retrieval of Mara's body? Was Andrew merely a pawn in a larger game, or worse, a mole? These thoughts fueled Omondi's resolve. Knowledge of this surveillance was kept on a need-to-know basis, and only his tight-knit team of three knew about the operation.

As he watched the house, he was determined to take as long as needed to build an airtight case. The patience of a predator was required, waiting for the prey to slip. Soon, he hoped, Thuku Waweru or his accomplices would make a mistake. And when they did, Omondi would be ready.

Back at home, Andrew dialed Inspector Omondi's number, hoping for an update. The inspector's voice was tense. "All the evidence is gone. The body, the photographs—everything. It's like they vanished overnight."

Andrew felt a chill. He had considered sharing his suspicions from the party with Omondi but held back. Without evidence, it would sound like paranoia. Omondi's next words were a further blow. "I'm dropping the case officially. There's nothing left to go on. I'm also seeking a transfer to Kisumu to be closer to my family."

"Goodbye, Andrew. I wish you all the best," Omondi said, his voice tinged with finality.

Hanging up, Andrew's mind raced. He called Angela Nyerere, the reporter, but couldn't reach her. Days passed without any response. Then, one evening, the news reported her death—found lifeless in her home, no signs of foul play. The housekeeper, who had been on leave, discovered her body.

Andrew knew it was no coincidence. The Architect had struck again, eliminating another threat. The reality of what he was up against sank in. This was a battle he couldn't win alone. He pondered his options, feeling a sense of hopelessness. Perhaps it was better to return to his normal life, to protect his family and let this dark chapter close.

As the storm clouds gathered, both metaphorically and literally, each character was left to ponder their next move. The battle lines were drawn, but the war was far from over. In the shadows, Inspector Omondi planned his next steps, while Charlene reveled in her apparent victory. Andrew, caught in the middle, faced a choice—fight against an unseen enemy or retreat to safeguard his loved ones.

The Architect's last laugh echoed in the quiet of the night, but it was uncertain who would have the final say. The game was still afoot, and the pieces were yet to make their decisive moves.

There is more to this story, and it is all in the next book "Shadows Behind The Light." What things would we do for wealth, are you ready for the sequel?

Appendix A: Timeline of Key Events

Introduction

- The doctor's initial foray into online dating

- Conversations with his friend Larry about the allure of dating apps

The Kidnapping

- The doctor's date with Mara

- The sudden drugging and abduction

- The doctor's harrowing experience in captivity

- The mysterious escape and subsequent confusion

The Aftermath

- The doctor's decision to tone down his activism following Sally's advice

- The family's holiday trip providing a semblance of normalcy
- Inspector Omondi's investigation and the leads pointing to Marcus

The Investigation

- Marcus's desperate call to Inspector Omondi
- The meeting and subsequent events leading to Marcus's death
- The discovery of Mara's body and the missing evidence

Unraveling Secrets

- The doctor's growing suspicion during the family gathering
- The revelation of Thuku Waweru's alias as "The Master" and Charlene as "The Architect"
- The doctor's struggle with the realization of his family's involvement

The Final Moves

- Inspector Omondi's secret task force and continued investigation

- The doctor's contact with the reporter and her untimely death

- The package with the bullet as a warning to Inspector Omondi

---

Glossary

- **Dark Web**: A part of the internet that is not indexed by search engines and is often used for illicit activities.

- **Phantom**: The alias of a highly skilled sniper and assassin.

- **Safe House**: A secret location used to hide and protect individuals.

- **Interpol**: The International Criminal Police Organization that facilitates international police cooperation.

- **Matatu**: A privately owned minibus or shared taxi in Kenya.

- **Nairobi**: The capital city of Kenya, where much of the story takes place.

- **Kisumu:** A city in Kenya where Inspector Omondi is purportedly transferred.

Bibliography/References

This book draws inspiration from various real-world elements and integrates them into its fictional narrative.

Index

- The Architect

- Thuku Waweru

- Timeline

Author Bio

Dr. Nicholas Okumu is a practicing surgeon, business owner, and advocate for surgical access. With a passion for storytelling, Dr. Okumu has woven a thrilling narrative that explores the dark underbelly of the digital world. Inspired by African literary greats and historical figures, Dr. Okumu blends real-world issues with gripping fiction. When not writing, Dr. Okumu dedicates time to family and various professional endeavors, always striving to make a positive impact on the community.

ISBN: 979-8-9911208-3-8